The Best of Spicy MYSTERY

Volume 2

The Best of Spicy Mystery

Volume 2

BY

ELLERY WATSON CALDER
HUGH SPEER
ROBERT LESLIE BELLEM
CLINT MORGAN
CLIVE TRENT
JEROME SEVERS PERRY
CARL MOORE
CARY MORAN
CLARK NELSON

EDITED BY

ALFRED JAN

ALTUS
PRESS

BOSTON

ALTUS PRESS

2015

EDITED AND DESIGNED BY

Matthew Moring

PUBLISHING HISTORY

"Spicy Mysteries Re-Examined" Copyright © 2012, 2015 Alfred Jan.

"Cats of Cassandra" originally appeared in the August, 1935 issue of *Spicy Mystery Stories*.

"Castle Sinister" originally appeared in the October, 1935 issue of *Spicy Mystery Stories*.

"She Who Was He!" originally appeared in the December, 1935 issue of *Spicy Mystery Stories*.

"Labyrinth of Monsters" originally appeared in the January, 1936 issue of *Spicy Mystery Stories*.

"Taupoo Dance" originally appeared in the April, 1936 issue of *Spicy Mystery Stories*.

"Blind Flight" originally appeared in the August, 1936 issue of *Spicy Mystery Stories*.

"The Secret of Old Farm" originally appeared in the September, 1936 issue of *Spicy Mystery Stories*.

"I Must Have 5 Corpses" originally appeared in the November, 1936 issue of *Spicy Mystery Stories*.

"False Face" originally appeared in the March, 1937 issue of *Spicy Mystery Stories*.

"Red—For Murder" originally appeared in the August, 1937 issue of *Spicy Mystery Stories*.

"Flesh of the Living" originally appeared in the October, 1939 issue of *Spicy Mystery Stories*.

THANKS TO

Chad Calkins, Alfred Jan & Jonathan Sweet

TABLE OF CONTENTS

ALFRED JAN

*O**f the four** titles in Culture Publication's spicy stable, *Spicy Mystery Stories* is the most unique and notorious. The first newsstand copy, dated June 1935, appeared third in the roster after *Spicy Adventure Stories,* November 1934, and *Spicy Detective Stories,* April 1934. *Spicy Western Stories,* November 1936, seemed to be an afterthought.

Spicy Mystery Stories stands out because the three men in charge, Lawrence Cadman, editor, Frank Armer, editor-in-chief, and publisher Harry Donenfeld, individually or collectively, exempted it from the boxed star treatment. During 1936 and 1937, all the other Spicys came out in unexpurgated and expurgated versions whose interior illustrations of women's bodies revealed less flesh, supported by textual changes reflecting this difference. A boxed star placed on the front cover's upper right-hand corner signified this censorship, leaving identical front cover paintings. The only nod to image taming in *Spicy Mystery Stories,* oddly enough, occurs on front covers: the woman in underwear on the June 1935 cover reappears in a dress on the June 1939 cover. Otherwise, graphic descriptions of female bodies coupled with salacious illustrations jump off the page in full force to stimulate male sexual fantasies, hence the notoriety. This clean and sexy strategy was unique among pulp magazine publishers. For a more complete discussion of Culture-Trojan self-censorship, see my essay in *Windy City Pulp Stories* #9, 2009, Black Dog Books, the best compilation of articles on the Spicy pulps to date.

I conceived this project to highlight worthy stories which rise above the warmed over weird menace category found in pulps like *Horror Stories, Terror Tales, Dime Mystery, Uncanny Tales, Thrilling Mystery,* and others. Containing the most formulaic of pulp story plots, they consist of a villain, usually a mad scientist, unscrupulous physician, greedy trust fund manager or land owner trying to achieve nefarious ends by scaring individuals or populations with seemingly supernatural phenomena which turn out in the end not to be; it was just Uncle Charley in a rubber monster suit and phosphorescent paint. After the villain is defeated and exposed by the hero, who always gets knocked unconscious by mid-plot, he and his female companion ride off in the daylight. Endings are always happy. Unfortunately, much of the content in *Spicy Mystery Stories* also fits this description.

On the other hand, this anthology is different. A major theme concerns consequences of overzealous American archeologists who knowingly or unknowingly violate sacred artefacts or people of Third World cultures. Viewed another way, what happens when spicy adventurers come home? Another story shows what can happen when a man falls too hard for a seductive woman. I included a locked-room murder mystery, an unusual find in this title. Henry Kuttner, the famous science fiction author, contributes a semi-weird menace tale to show his thematic breadth. Hugh B. Cave (Justin Case) writes about avenging past wrongs, with a twist ending, and as far as I know, this story has never been reprinted.

Malibu Graphics published the last *Spicy Mystery Stories* anthology in 1990, so it is time to take another look. Most pulp fans collect it for the covers and their rarity, but not for the stories. However, I believe more gems can be found between its covers, and if this volume generates sufficient interest, I anticipate bringing more to light for contemporary readers to enjoy.

In this second volume of *The Best of Spicy Mystery,* I want to bring out the variety of themes anchoring both supernatural and weird menace plots, acknowledging the latter can be more creative than typical mundane versions. A prime example is "Labyrinth of Monsters" by Robert Leslie Bellem. First reprinted 43 years ago in Tony Goodstone's anthology, its starkly gruesome imagery merits a repeat appearance. Although genetic birth defects are sensitively treated today, they were horror devices back then, and when combined with salacious physical female attributes, a potent brew was concocted indeed.

Strong women and femme fatales appeared quite often, despite the excess of woman victim cover paintings. Cats as witch familiars are common in folklore, as in "Cats of Cassandra" where they avenge her death. In addition, the June 1936 cover features a snarling cat paired with an evil woman sporting cat claws for fingernails, hardly a portrayal of weakness. A deadly femme fatale manipulates men in "False Face," and women defeat a male killer of females in "Red—For Murder."

Gender bending, an unusual subject, manifests in "She Who Was He!" and "Castle Sinister," which hints at Robert Bloch's novel and Alfred Hitchcock's movie, *Psycho*. Another example, anticipating a much later horror film from the early 1980s, is Clive Trent's "The Secret of Old Farm" and Frank Henenlotter's *Basket Case*.

Rounding out the anthology are stories about Chinese villainy, infectious disease, deranged love, and a ghost pilot flying a phantom plane, all served with a generous portion of spice!

A practicing optometrist, Alfred Jan has edited short fiction collections by D.L. Champion (with Bill Blackbeard), Robert Leslie Bellem, and Joel Townsley Rogers, and contributed articles on Norbert Davis, Cornell Woolrich, and other pulp-related topics to Blood 'N' Thunder *magazine. Alfred holds an M.A. in Philosophy, specializing in Aesthetics, and published freelance art criticism from 1982 to 1995. Work in progress includes a sample of works on ethics and aesthetics by the bohemian Gelett Burgess.*

ELLERY WATSON CALDER

CATS OF CASSANDRA

Her unearthly beauty was a snare to the wicked—her eerie companions were as weird as the fortune-teller herself… a slinking horde to suck the hot blood of death at last.

*T*HEY came at him like a soft, furry avalanche, so that he would have cried out had not some strange paralysis glued his tongue. From the doors they came, and from the dark corners. On softly-padded feet they sprang at him, silently like black ghosts, their green eyes glowing lambent fire. They were as creatures from hell, and their number was unending. Without sound and without warning they appeared; they were a dark tide of living movement, and they came toward him.

He shrank backward from their advance, and a great fear filled him. He found the door through which he had entered, and he fumbled at the knob. Then cold moisture beaded his forehead, and trembled with a sudden, nauseating terror; for the door was strangely locked, so that he could not flee.

The furry, silent horde was close to him now. A gulping sob rasped within his constricted throat, and dread panic seized at his heart. Like a nightmare it seemed to him—the gloom-veiled, sinister house, the unlocked door that had invited his entrance, the sudden realization that he was trapped. Yet it was real—horribly real. The house was real; the oncoming, silent avalanche was real. Green eyes burned into his brain.

And then, at a far doorway, there was suddenly Cassandra.

She spoke a command; and her voice was like a deep-throated purr. At her bidding, the furry tide halted.

She smiled at Mort Marriner. "You are afraid of my cats?" she asked him quietly.

He found his voice. It trembled strangely in his throat. "I—yes,

"You need not fear,"
the vision said; "they
will do you no harm."

I was—afraid—"

"You need no longer fear. They will do you no harm." She came toward him, and her movement was silent, with a feline grace.

HE tore his eyes away from the furry things at his feet, and his gaze rested upon the girl who drew near to him. The garment that covered her was a flowing thing of some queer, almost trans-

lucent material that shimmered greenly in the semi-dark. Through it he could discern the smooth, catlike litheness of her body, and the rounded promontories of her breasts.

He looked into her eyes, and his own grew wide with wonderment. Her pupils were dark vertical slits in irises of green, and it seemed to him that her eyes glowed strangely in the gloom. She smiled once more, and her white teeth were pointed and sharp with a feline sharpness.

Abruptly he knew that he was afraid of her.

It was as though she had divined his fear, for she said, "I mean you no harm. I would only ask what you want of me."

Her long, white-tapered hands hung at her sides. He saw the crimson splashes that were her sharp fingernails, and they reminded him of claws that had been dipped deep in blood…. He shuddered, and his mind sought for a plausible excuse for his being in that somber house.

Then he remembered the dim sign outside. In the baleful white gleam of the full moon he had read it: "Madame Cassandra, Seeress." Now he licked his parched lips. He dared not tell her that he had found her front door unlocked; that he had entered silent and unbidden, with robbery in his heart. Instead, he croaked a craven's lie. "I—my name's Mort Marriner. I came here to see Madame Cassandra to have my fortune told. I rang the bell, but no one answered. Then I found the front door unlocked, and came in."

The girl in shimmering green smiled softly. "You wish Madame Cassandra to read your future?" she purred in her flawless throat,

"Yes. Is—is she in?" Desperately he hoped that her answer would be negative, so that he could leave this place.

The girl said, "I am Cassandra."

He stared at her, for the moment confused. "But—you are too young—!"

"I am Cassandra," she repeated. She touched his arm, and a cold wind seemed to blow through the crevices of his mean soul. "Come," she said slowly. "Come with me."

Unwillingly he followed her, back into a smaller room where green lights flickered ghoulishly. And although he did not look back, he knew that the furry horde was at his heels—silent, watchful, like flitting shadows.

In a huge chair Cassandra seated herself, so that the flickering green lights were reflected in her strange eyes. On the table before her was a huge crystal in which the green lights danced deeply, like imprisoned ghosts of fire. Green lights and green eyes and flickering green fires seared deep into Mort Marriner's brain, and his hands were cold.

He felt a furry thing rub against his leg, and sharp claws bit at his flesh suddenly. He cried out, in a voice loud with terror. Cassandra smiled and spoke in a strange, slurred tongue that he did not, could not comprehend.

Then her gaze flickered across his corpse-white features, and her purring tone was warm-reassuring. "I have told them that you are my friend. They understand now, and will not alarm you more."

He tried to answer her; tried to tell her that he no longer sought a forecast of his future. He tried to tell her that he wanted, desperately, to leave. But once more that strange paralysis locked his tongue, and he was silent.

Cassandra's cat eyes went dreamily to the green-glowing crystal. It was as though he had not been there with her in the room.

LONG she stared into the gleaming globe; and there seemed to be a purring sound deep in her throat. Her black hair streamed down over her shoulders like an inky waterfall, and her breasts were perfect beneath the translucence of her shimmering emerald garment. And then, dreamily, she spoke as though from a far, distant place.

"The story of Cassandra is a story of tragedy," she said slowly.

"Of—of Cassandra?" Mort Marriner spoke the words thickly.

"Cassandra was daughter to Priam, King of Troy. She was the beloved of Apollo, who gave to her the gift of prophesy. Love is a strange thing, my friend. Apollo's died. He became angry with Cassandra. And because he could not take from her the gift of prophesy which he had bestowed upon her, he decreed a bitter thing. He decreed that henceforth no living man should believe the things she prophesied." The girl sighed gently. "Cassandra was killed, afterward, in the sacking of Troy."

Mort Marriner wiped the cold moisture from his forehead, and his question was thick-tongued. "But—what has that to do with me?" he choked.

"Only this, my friend. The things I see within this crystal are things that will inevitably come to pass; and yet you will not believe them."

"You—see things in the crystal?" He stared into the gleaming iridescent globe, but his eyes encountered naught save flickering, imprisoned green lights…

"I see many things in the crystal," she answered. "I see that you came here to rob me, because you had heard whisperings of the treasure I possess."

"It's—it's—" He tried to tell her it was a lie, but the untruth lodged in his throat and would not utter. He was silent and abruptly ashamed. And he was frightened with a nameless dread.

Her green eyes swept his face, and then they returned to the emerald-gleaming crystal ball. "There are ominous things in store for you, Mort Marriner," she said. "And… for me. Yet before these events come to pass there will be a brief moment of intoxication—of rapture—"

"I—I don't want to hear any more!" he cried out.

"But you will hear until the end, Mort Marriner. You will stay, and you will hear, because it has been written thus since time began."

"God!" he whispered.

Again she gazed deep into the crystal. "I see strange things," she purred huskily. "I see—" abruptly her voice choked off, and her face went white. She pushed the crystal globe from her, and her crimson-tipped fingers trembled strangely. She arose, and the grace of her body was feline, cat-like. Her hand went to her breast, pressed into the firm-resilient flesh through the translucent stuff of her robe as though to still a sudden beating of her heart. And as Mort Marriner's fascinated eyes followed her gesture, he suddenly lost all fear.

Instead, there surged up within him a desire for her that licked at his veins like green fire. It was queer, he thought, that his terror of her should thus be transformed into desire; yet it must have been inevitably so, for she was beautiful with a weird and unearthly beauty that transcended mortal perfection.

Her mouth was crimson-ripe with kisses to be harvested, and

her body was made for the embrace of passion. Her hips were sinuously curved, and her bosoms were twin dreams that cried out for his caresses. One step he took toward her.

SHE smiled into his eyes, and her hand brushed his arm. This time it was no cold wind that froze the crevices of his soul, but a hot gusty storm that filled him with aching and longing.

"Come, Mort Marriner," she said. "I will show you the treasure you had hoped to steal."

And now he followed her willingly, eagerly; nor did he think of the pad-padding, furry things that flowed like a living tide at his heels. She led him up a dim stairway, and they entered a perfumed room.

She went to a grotesque-carven chest. As though by some magic its lid flew up at her touch.

Her blood-red fingers dipped into the chest's interior, and when she withdrew her hands they were draped with scintillant gems that glistened and glittered and gleamed. There were diamonds and rubies as red as warm-flowing blood, and there were emeralds that glowed green like the eyes of a cat... like the eyes of Cassandra. At the sight of them Mort Marriner drew his breath, painful-sharply.

And then he knew that he had no desire for the jewels; knew that this girl in the green translucent garment was the only thing in that dim house that he wanted. He went to her, and his hands disentangled the ropes of gems from her fingers so that they slid back glisteningly into the chest, with tiny clatter-noises.

She faced him, and very slowly he reached up to unfasten the shimmering robe where it was caught together at her neck. A light flared into her eyes as the sleazy drape rippled to the floor. Then she stood before him in glorious nakedness, and reverently he drank in the glories of her body with his eyes.

He touched her, suddenly fearful that so much perfection be not real. Her flesh was warm to his fingers; her breasts throbbed like captive things beneath his palms. He kissed her.

She fused against his body like a vibrant reed, and he could feel the quivering tremble of her in his hard arms. Then he picked her up gently, although his veins seethed and bubbled with hot passion; and he kissed her neck, her shoulders, as though he had been long-starved for the taste of her flesh….

By some necromancy they were together upon a cushioned divan, silk-soft and passion-warm. Her arms were about his neck, and her blood-red lips parted once more for his ardent-questing kiss. He felt the tip of her tongue; *it was rough, scratchy, like a cat's!*

Abruptly a cold, wintry chill seemed to freeze his marrow, and he stared into her green-irised eyes that were like a cat's eyes. She smiled, and her sharp-pointed teeth were like cat's teeth. Her black hair had fallen away from her face, and as he saw her ears he felt suddenly sick, then suddenly red-raging. *Her ears were soft and furry and pointed—like cat's ears!*

He could not fathom the abrupt fury that surged in him; could not plumb the insane and frenetic fear that made him leap up from her warm side. It was as though he had gone out of his body, and a raging demon had entered. As though in an anger-ridden nightmare he felt his hand go to the knife at his belt, saw the blade glitter in the dim light as he brought it plunging down into the white flesh of her throat….

AND then he came to his senses, and flung the intruding demon from him. Like waves beating against his brain came the reiterated knowledge, over and over a thousand times. He had killed Cassandra, and she was dead.

He looked at her, and then he closed his eyes weakly. The knife still quivered in her warm throat, and red blood streamed over the cushioned divan, crimson-staining and murder-accusing.

Slowly he gripped himself; slowly and cautiously he edged away from her lovely lifeless corpse. He must get away, he said. He must escape, he told himself. He must leave this ghastly house, he whispered.

Why had he killed Cassandra? He did not know. He knew only that suddenly he had hated her; had hated her feline body and her cat's eyes and furry, pointed ears with a consuming hatred. It was as though his hatred had been a thing apart from him—predestined from the beginning of time….

The knife stuck horribly in her throat, mocking him as he picked up the jewels.

"It has been written thus since time began"—that was what Cassandra had told him, when she had looked into the green-glowing crystal. A cold sweat stood out on his forehead and made his body wet, cold. Was it this she had meant when she had predicted an hour of intoxication, of bliss, for them both—before ominous things overshadowed them?

He shook himself, forced himself to laugh aloud in that silent murder-room. He was being a fool! There need be nothing ominous ahead of him—if he was very careful. He would get away, go to some far place, forget this night of miasmatic nightmare. But… he had no money. How could he journey to a far place without money?

Then he smiled. Why had he come here in the first place? Because he had intended to steal Cassandra's jewels! Well, the carven chest was still open, and Cassandra had no further need of them—

He leaped to the chest, stuffed his pockets with the glittering baubles until his coat bulged pregnantly. Then, resolutely his eyes avoiding the bleeding thing on the divan, he left the room and stole softly down the stairs.

He reached the lower hall. He frowned. He had forgotten something. What was it? He could not remember. Then, suddenly he did remember.

He remembered because it was written since the beginning of time. And the thing he remembered was—that furry avalanche, fiery-eyed and silent-footed!

They were coming toward him. He would have cried out had not some strange paralysis glued his tongue. From the hallway they came, and from the dark corners. On softly-padded feet they sprang at him, silently like black ghosts, their green eyes glowing lambent fire. And then they were upon him.

He beat at them frantically, his terrified hands striking into their furry midst. Their sharp claws tore at his fingers, stripped the flesh from the bones of his wrists and arms. Their sharp feline teeth were at his legs, so that he could feel his hot life-blood draining from him.

He went to his knees in that silent feline welter. Needle-sharp claws lacerated his cheeks and sank gruesomely into his eyeballs....

Hell-blackness overtook him, and he died.

* * * *

From the Evening Bulletin, Feb. 15, 193—

FIND SKELETON IN HOUSE; WOMAN MISSING

Attracted by the strange yowling of cats, Patrolman Dennis Lafferty today forced his way into a house at 1677 N. Aldama

Street and stumbled upon a gruesome find. In the lower hallway was the skeleton of a man, the flesh completely gone from
the bones.

The house, which had been occupied by a woman known only as
"Cassandra," a mystic and fortune-teller, was unoccupied except
for a horde of black cats whose noise had attracted the policeman. Cassandra herself was not at home, and up until a late hour
this afternoon had not been located by the police.

A strange factor in the mystery lies in the discovery, in a room
on the second floor, of the body of a huge black cat. The animal
was dead. It had a dagger in its throat.

CASTLE SINISTER

A living substitute for the corpse that
had been a madman's toy! Such was the
fate offered the girl who crossed the castle
drawbridge—and burned it behind her.

MARCIA LUDLOW descended from the vestibule of the day-coach, carrying her single suitcase. In the waning light of the grey, overcast afternoon she stood uncertainly on the tiny station's platform as the train pulled out. There was something depressing about her surroundings; an inexplicable atmosphere of gloom that seemed to close in around her and to blanket her.

Marcia was very lovely, and her inexpensive, ill-fitting dress could not disguise the lilting, feminine curves and contours of her youthful figure. The gold of her hair was like the pale dawn, and the azure of her eyes matched the skies of a summer evening.

Her lips were crimson, kissable; but just now they held a faint tremulousness which she seemed unable to control.

As she stared about her, she suddenly heard footfalls approaching from behind. Nervously she turned. She saw a tall, erect man smiling at her. He was clad in subdued livery that emphasized the muscularity of his shoulders, the athletic hardness of his body. He bowed a little. "Miss Ludlow?" he spoke inquiringly.

"Yes. I'm Marcia Ludlow."

"I'm Winston, Miss Gregory's chauffeur. She sent me to pick you up and bring you to Castle Gregory."

The chauffeur's voice was low and resonant; and somehow his very presence seemed to dispel the depressing gloom of the dying day. Marcia Ludlow smiled at him. "Thank you," she said shyly. "I was beginning to think maybe Miss Gregory had forgotten me."

Winston, the chauffeur, made no answer; but Marcia thought she detected a queer flicker in his dark eyes at her words. He took her bag, carried it toward a waiting, somber sedan which seemed to Marcia a little like a hearse… although she couldn't fathom the reason for such a weird impression.

ABRUPTLY, the tall chauffeur turned to Marcia, just before he placed her suitcase in the sedan's tonneau. "Miss Gregory engaged you as her secretary, didn't she? By mail?"

Marcia nodded. "Yes. To both questions. Why do you ask?"

He looked searchingly into her eyes. "How badly do you need the job?"

There was no hint of impertinence to his tone. Rather, it seemed as if he had taken a sudden, deeply-personal interest which sent a tiny darting sensation of gratitude through Marcia's heart. She smiled. "I need the job very much. Need it terribly."

"You'd be better off if you didn't take it," Winston said in a curiously flat voice.

Marcia drew a sharp breath, so that her firm little breasts swelled outward like twin, sharp-pointed cones through her frock. "What do you mean?" she exclaimed.

He looked at her gravely. "If I gave you the money to buy a ticket back to the city, would you go?"

Marcia stared at the man. "I—I don't understand. And certainly I wouldn't pass up a good job—"

"No. I suppose not," he answered her. "Forgive me." He placed her bag in the back of the car, assisted her into the front seat beside his own. As he slipped behind the steering wheel and tooled the heavy sedan in a circle, Marcia studied his strong profile.

His lips were grim, and there was a certain hardness to his jutting jaw… as though he might be facing some approaching strife.

It was then that Marcia Ludlow knew sudden fear—a vague, unvoiced fear of impending danger. But the presence of Winston, the chauffeur, beside her, was like a steadying hand. Abruptly she was glad that he would be working in the same household with her.

Marcia gasped as she peered into that chamber. God in Heaven! Could such things be?

IN silence he drove for a long time, through the gathering gloom. The road twisted snake-like along the side of the mountain; and deep in the ravine below, somber shadows thickened over the stunted trees and underbrush which lined the banks of a fetid, slow-moving stream. The wax-white blossoms of locust trees along the roadway sent a sweet, cloying fragrance through the dusk…. Like flowers at a funeral, Marcia found herself thinking….

The road dipped suddenly; plunged precipitously and sinuously into the ravine below. Then, around an abrupt bend, Marcia caught her first glimpse of Castle Gregory, where she was to be employed.

It was a vast structure of moss-covered, ivy-ridden grey stone. There were looming, turreted towers at all four corners; and the entire building seemed to frown and glower at the valley in which it stood rooted.

There was a green-scummed, turgid moat surrounding the place, heightening the medieval illusion. A drawbridge was lowered across the moat, giving access to the castle's courtyard.

Marcia knew something of Castle Gregory's history. Years ago it had been rebuilt, stone by stone, from the ruins of an ancient castle in England—ruins which had been transported to America and erected by Colonel Lawrence Gregory, a retired army officer.

He had built the place for his new bride. But a few months later, the young wife had eloped with a lover; and Colonel Gregory had become a somber recluse until the day of his death, three years ago.

Since that time, the castle had been occupied by the dead man's sister, Miss Georgine Gregory, an elderly spinster. It was this

*There was nothing
she could do but lie
there and watch that
battle to a finish.*

woman for whom Marcia Ludlow was now to work.

Marcia stared at the sinister castle as Winston, the chauffeur, slowed the sedan's speed and headed toward the lowered drawbridge. Studying the nearest rounded tower, she noticed that its windows were all barred. And then, abruptly, Marcia stiffened in her seat.

Was it an illusion born of the dusk—or had she actually seen a pale, feminine face at one of those barred windows? For a single instant it had been there—a face in which terror, horror, had stamped impending insanity. Then, like a flash, it was gone.

Marcia's hand went to the chauffeur's forearm. "Look—that tower window!" she whispered.

He followed her gaze. This time there was no question about it; there *was* a face at the barred window! But not the feminine face Marcia had first seen. This was a grotesque, leering, horrifying face—a man's face! Misshapen, sinister, bestially ugly… like a nightmare-fiend out of hell! And it glared down from the window at the approaching sedan; glared, while its lips curled back from tusk-like fangs, and clawing fingers writhed on the bars of the window like twisting, curling snakes….

"God—what was that thing?" Marcia Ludlow whispered tensely. Suddenly she crouched against the hard body of the chauffeur. "I—*I'm afraid!*" she gasped out.

His right hand left the wheel; his arm encircled her waist gently. The touch of his hand subdued the tremors which had shaken Marcia's body. "Take it easy!" he cautioned her. "There's no cause for alarm—yet. In due time you'll find out what—and who—it was you saw at the window. Meanwhile, pretend you didn't see it. It will be better that way."

"But—but what—!" Marcia whispered.

"I can't tell you anything just now, my dear. But in case… anything happens to frighten you, call for me. Tod Winston. I'll be somewhere nearby. I promise you that."

"Th-thank you, Tod Winston," Marcia answered slowly.

AND then the hearse-like sedan had crossed the drawbridge, entered the castle's courtyard. Winston took Marcia's bag and assisted Marcia out of the car. He guided her into the house—into a vast, high-vaulted main hall.

The room was pure Gothic; dark, smoke-blackened wooden arches and beams formed the ceiling, and the floor was of uneven flags. There was a damp chill to the air, and the gloom was dispelled only by such flickering, spectral light as came from a leaping fire on the great hearth at the far end of the hall.

Marcia stared about her, dubiously. The dancing shadows from the fire made everything seem weird and unreal. Even the lean, strong features of Tod Winston, the chauffeur, seemed transformed by the yellow-flaming illumination. For an instant he seemed somehow sinister, demon-like.

But the sensation passed when he smiled. "Stay here," he said to Marcia. "I'll go summon Miss Gregory and tell her you're here."

He left Marcia, went through a frowning, heavy doorway. And as he closed the great oak portal behind him, Marcia suddenly heard a sound that froze the marrow in her bones. It was a hellish, inhuman, unearthly ululation—the insane, frenetic laughter of a mindless fiend!

It rasped on Marcia's eardrums like a hacksaw through living bone; it knifed into her consciousness with terrifying sharpness, curdling her blood and sending slithering crawls of fear through her flesh. Again it sounded—a penetrating crescendo of mad laughter which ended abruptly, unexpectedly, in a choked shriek of pain and of fear. Then silence—utter, brooding, somber silence broken only by the hissing, crackling sound of the fire on the hearth….

"Well, my dear! Welcome to Castle Gregory!" a smooth voice said.

Marcia whirled, white-faced. She stared at a woman who had entered the vast hall so soundlessly as to be unheard until this instant. A tall, spare woman, modishly dressed in a prim, severe fashion; a woman with iron-grey hair, kindly features, smiling eyes, and an angular, almost masculine figure.

Marcia's hand went to her swelling left breast. "Oh—!" she gasped.

The grey-haired woman smiled. "Did I frighten you? I'm sorry, my dear. Forgive me. I'm Miss Gregory. And you, of course, are Marcia Ludlow, my new secretary."

Marcia took a swift step toward the older woman. "I—yes. I'm Marcia Ludlow. But—but I think I've changed my mind about staying here. I—I believe I'd rather go back to the city."

"Nonsense!" Miss Gregory smiled. "Something's frightened you. Was it that laughter you just heard?"

"Y-yes."

"Forget it, my dear. That was merely my poor dead brother's unfortunate valet. The chap was shell-shocked during the war; and when my brother retired, he brought the man with him as his personal servant. Soon afterward, the fellow's mind gave way entirely.

"When my brother died, he stipulated in his will that the madman be given refuge and sanctuary here as long as he lived. We keep the poor fellow locked in a top room of the west tower. He's harmless enough—and he's under lock and key constantly."

"Oh… I see," Marcia nodded. So that explained the leering, maniacal face at the barred window of the tower. But—but what about that other face she had seen? That corpse-white, fear-tortured woman's face…? Or had Marcia merely imagined she had seen it?

"You're tired and hungry, Marcia, my dear," the older woman smiled gently. "Come—I'll give you a bite to eat and then show you to your room. You'll want a good night's rest. Tomorrow will be time enough to explain your new duties." She took Marcia's arm, led her into a smaller room. Supper was already on the table. They ate.

LATER, Marcia followed her new employer up a flight of winding, steep stone steps that led upward into one of the towers. Miss Gregory unlocked a door, switched on the lights. Marcia saw a small, circular, comfortable chamber, pleasantly furnished.

There was a great, ancient four-poster bed, snowy and crisp with fresh linens.

"Good night, my dear. Sleep well," the grey-haired Miss Gregory said in her kindly, husky voice. Then she left Marcia alone in the room, closing the door behind her.

Marcia heard the woman's sharp, decisive footsteps descending the winding stone staircase within the well of the tower; and a sudden sensation of vague, unutterable uneasiness assailed her. She tried to throw the feeling off by busying herself with the unpacking of her suitcase.

Then she disrobed, shrugging out of her dress and peeling off her tissue-thin step-ins, her hose, her shoes. For a brief instant she stood there, entirely nude, gloriously feminine. Her lilting, unbrassiered breasts were smooth domes of loveliness; her unclad body was a symphonic tone-poem in girl-flesh. The flat plateau of her stomach blended into the slimly-lush curvatures of her hips; her thighs were cream-smooth, blemishless; her legs were tapered and delicately-contoured.

She donned a sheer, gossamer sleeping-gown; went toward the bed. Then she hesitated. Again she experienced that strange sensation of vague uneasiness, of impending evil. Abruptly it seemed as though the circular walls of her chamber were closing in upon her, slowly, implacably.…

On sudden impulse she sprang toward the closed door of her room. She had to get out of here—she must! A nameless fear hovered over her, mocking, gibbering, whispering…. She gained the door, wrenched at the knob. And then her face went white.

The door was locked—*from the outside!* Marcia was a prisoner!

And even as she made the discovery, the light in her room suddenly flickered and went out!

DARKNESS, solid, impenetrable, closed down about Marcia Ludlow like a smothering shroud, choking her, stifling her so that the cry of terror which issued from her lips was only a harsh, despairing whisper. Again she wrenched at the doorknob; without result!

Then she turned, stumbled blindly through the darkness toward the far wall of the circular room. At last she gained the chamber's only window. Its shade was drawn. She tugged at it, and it shot upon its spring-roller with a sharp, rattling snap. Marcia blanched. The window was barred with heavy, close-set steel rods….

She stared outward through the imprisoning bars. The clouds had drifted away from the valley, unveiling a round, sneering moon that glared malevolently down like the eye of a huge demon. Marcia saw the courtyard below, bathed in the malefic white glare. Nothing stirred, nothing moved below her.

It was as though she looked upon the silence of an open tomb…. The cracks which split the courtyard's paving seemed like black, writhing snakes frozen into immobility as they had tried to slither toward the black, yawning hole of an open, long-unused well.

Tap! Tap! Tap!

Marcia tensed. What was that sound? Again it came—a faint, muffled, subdued tapping. But where? Then she realized that someone was knocking a muffled tattoo upon her locked door!

In the etiolated moonlight which glared in through her barred window, Marcia turned, raced toward the door. "Who's there?" she whispered from her constricted throat.

"Marcia—Marcia Ludlow! Are you in there?"

"Y-yes! Who is it?"

*He lifted the corpse high,
poised it, threw it far....*

"It's Tod Winston—the chauffeur."

A sudden, leaping relief flooded Marcia's veins. "I—I'm locked in here! I can't get out!" she cried through the imprisoning door.

"1 know that. I've got a key. Wait a minute." Winston's voice was calm, reassuring. Marcia crouched; heard the rasping of metal against metal. Then, abruptly, the door swung open on smoothly-oiled, silent hinges.

A shadowy, tall figure leaped into the room. Marcia saw Tod Winston's strong, tense features. He stared at her. "You're... all right? Nothing's happened to you?" he demanded.

"N-no. Except that... someone locked me in...."

HIS dark eyes seemed to gleam for an instant as he surveyed her. Through the thinness of her night-gown he could see the sweeping curves of her hips, the rise of her firm young breasts, limned in the searching moonlight. Then, because she had been so desperately afraid, and because now she was so utterly relieved, Marcia crept close to Tod Winston; felt his arms go about her gently, protectively….

For a long moment he held her; and his muscles quivered and sang with the nearness of her warm young body. "My dear!" he whispered…. Then his face grew somber, grave. "I've got to get you out of here! You're in danger—bad danger!"

"Wh-what do you mean—?" Marcia drew a sharp breath. Once more she felt fear creeping through her, chilling her.

He looked into her eyes. "Tell me. Have you a family—mother, father, anyone?"

Marcia shook her head. "N-no. Nobody. Why do you ask?"

He would not answer her question. Instead, his lips compressed into a grim line. "Listen!" he whispered. "You stay right here. Close the door. Bar it with the bed—with anything. I'm going down to get the sedan out of the garage and across the drawbridge. Then I'll come back for you. Don't open the door for anybody except me! Understand?"

"Y-yes."

"Good!" He turned to leave her. Then, unexpectedly, he whirled and caught her in his strong arms. One hand cupped her breast, thrillingly, adoringly. He kissed her parted lips….

Then he had gone!

Marcia closed the door after him; stood there waiting a brief moment. Suddenly she heard something that brought maggots of fear into her veins and congealing ice to her spine.

It was a weird, hell-born shriek of insane agony, of crystalline terror…. And it came from somewhere within that very tower which held Marcia Ludlow's room!

"Oh, God!" Marcia cried out. Had someone—or *something*—struck Tod Winston from behind, killed him…? Marcia flung open her door, leaped out into the darkness of the tower. Again that blood-congealing shriek split the night. It came from above.

Marcia launched herself at the winding, circular stone staircase and started up—

She gained the top landing. There was a closed door before her; a door into which had been cut a small, square opening, barred with heavy steel rods. Light filtered out through the barred square—and on the wings of that light came a harsh, gibbering ululation—like the laughter of a slimy fiend from hell!

As though hypnotized, Marcia stared through the hole in the door. And then sudden horror-nausea clawed at her viscera. "God in heaven!" she moaned.

She was looking into a tiny, circular chamber lighted by a single, glaring incandescent bulb set high on the far wall. The room was utterly bare, save for a ragged cot—

And on the cot lay the limp, lifeless figure of a naked girl—a red-haired girl, utterly unclad, delicately lovely.... Or rather, she must have been lovely, once. But now....

MARCIA LUDLOW recognized the red-haired girl. It was the one whose terror-distorted face she had seen at the barred tower-window when first she had come to Castle Gregory. But the girl had been alive, then.... Now she was dead! Horribly, obscenely dead... murdered just a few short instants before!

Her flesh was ripped, lacerated, gashed as though by talons and fangs. A great, raw gout of flesh had been torn from her white throat, and spates of crimson blood fountained from severed jugular and carotid artery.... Gore spewed from the wound, trickled over the dead girl's mutilated breasts, stained the ragged cot with a spreading pool of thick crimson—

Marcia Ludlow swayed. Toward the cot, with its gruesome burden, a shambling, grotesque figure was moving.... A misshapen, inhuman form, twisted, hunched, utterly foul and fiendish.... Unshaven, its cheeks quivered horribly, and its red-rimmed eyes glared with sadistic, maniacal lust. Its loose lips slobbered, gibbered, dripped crimson froth. It sprang at the feminine corpse on the cot; sank its fangs deep into that mutilated throat....

Marcia swayed. That misshapen, grotesquely-hunched form— that was the madman whom Miss Gregory had mentioned! The insane servant who was supposed to be "harmless"! With a despairing cry, Marcia turned and staggered down the circular stone staircase, gained her own room, flung herself inside.

She slammed the door; braced herself against it, panting, terrified. Suppose that human beast—that unutterable monster—should come out of his lair, sneak down the stairs, try to break into Marcia's room…?

She fumbled at the door, seeking some key with which she might lock herself in. But there was none. Cold horror-sweat bathed her forehead, ran into her eyes, blinded her. She leaped toward the heavy four-poster bed, dragged it inch by inch toward the door until it stood in lieu of a lock.

What was that?

Footsteps were racing, ascending the stone staircase outside Marcia's room in the well of the stone tower. Heavy, masculine footsteps. They went past her landing, continued upward. Marcia crouched, listening. She heard a man's bellowing roar of rage; an answering shriek of insane frenzy. Then came the sounds of a scuffle.

Marcia heard a man's harsh voice saying, "You fool! I'll give you another one in exchange—one who's alive! Then you can kill again!"

Then, for a moment, there was silence; silence which was followed by a slithering, bumping sound on the staircase, as though someone were dragging a limp, lifeless burden…. Suddenly Marcia realized the truth. Somebody—a man—had gone into that upper room, taken the dead body of the mutilated red-haired girl from the clutches of the madman. And in taking the corpse, there had been a promise to replace it… with a living substitute!

Marcia felt an icy premonition gnawing at her vitals; a premonition that she, herself, was to be that substitute! That she was to be thrown to that madman—to be a victim of the maniac's murderous lust!

The slithering, bumping sound died away in the lower reaches of the tower. Marcia rose to her feet, staggered toward her barred window, stared outward and downward toward the moon-drenched courtyard below. And then a gasping sob rose to her lips. "God—oh, my God!" she shrieked.

A TALL, athletic figure had emerged from the castle, into the courtyard. A figure clad in subdued livery… and carrying a bloody white burden—the limp, lifeless corpse of the red-haired girl whom the madman had murdered! Marcia recognized the livery, and tentacles of terror wrapped about her heart, squeezed it dry of blood. It was a chauffeur's livery—the livery of Tod Winston!

She watched him, horror-stricken and silent. He crossed the courtyard, approached the yawning black mouth of that open, disused well. He lifted the corpse in his arms, poised it—and flung it into the hole, callously, fiendishly! Then he turned and raced back toward the entrance to the castle's main hall.

And then Marcia Ludlow realized why Tod Winston had questioned her about her family. He wanted to be sure that there would be nobody who'd make inquiries for her, if she disappeared… as that red-haired girl was now vanished from the earth! He intended to hand her over to the lusts of that fiendish madman; and when she was dead, he would throw her body into the well… even as he had just disposed of the red-haired girl's corpse!

Marcia sank to the floor of her room, her brain whirling, numbed, stupefied. Moments passed. And then she stiffened. Someone was tapping on her door!

"Marcia—let me in! It's Tod Winston! I've got the car out of its garage and across the moat. Come on, girl—quick!"

Marcia sprang toward the door, braced herself against the bed. "Go away!" she shrieked wildly. "Let me alone! I know what you want! You want that maniac to kill me—!"

She heard his answering gasp, surprised, sharp, rasping… "Marcia—for God's sake! Have you gone mad, girl? Let me in, I say! Hurry! There's no time to be lost!"

"No!" Marcia's voice rose to a shrill pitch of unadulterated terror. "I won't! You'll kill me—you'll give me to that madman!"

"You little fool!" his grating voice knifed through the closed door. And then he was battering at the portal, savagely, powerfully, with smashing force. Within the room, Marcia could hear

*"Drop that girl,
Winston, or you die!"*

the impact of his hard shoulders, time after time, as he plunged against the heavy woodwork, crashed into it.

In the moonlight which filtered through her barred, open window, Marcia could see the heavy door straining inward, forcing back the barricading four-poster bed. Viscid terror gripped her, paralyzed her.

She crouched against the floor, wide-eyed, staring, cowering; and she was afraid with a dread, numbing horror that held her in slime-crawling thralls. She was powerless, unable to move; she could not cry out—

The bed slithered across the floor toward her; the door smashed open. Tod Winston hurled himself into the room; saw Marcia; leaped at her. He snatched her into his arms. He whirled.

Marcia beat at him with her tiny, ineffectual fists. In her struggles, the neck of her night-robe ripped and split, baring her lovely breasts. The chauffeur held her grimly, mashing her against him, crushing her bosom flat upon his panting chest. His eyes were narrowed, strangely glinting—

And then the paralysis which had gripped Marcia's constricted throat, suddenly vanished. She screamed—a wild, shrieking crescendo of sound that gibbered through the night and through the tower, echoing and re-echoing like a banshee's tortured lamentation.

"Marcia—in the name of God—!" Tod Winston rasped harshly. His palm went to her open mouth, clamped over it, smothered her cries. But he was too late.

Already, footsteps were pounding swiftly up the circular stone staircase outside the room, within the well of the stone tower. And then, abruptly, Marcia saw the grey-haired Miss Gregory standing in the doorway—and the woman held a heavy automatic in her unwavering right hand!

"Winston—drop that girl!" The woman's sharp command was like a stinging whiplash.

THE chauffeur's shoulders slumped. Awkwardly he set Marcia on her feet. Then he faced Miss Gregory; and in the pallid moonglow, his face was curiously contorted. "You—!" he rasped.

The grey-haired woman jammed her automatic's muzzle against his thick chest. "Another word and you die, Winston!" she said evenly. Her lips were a thin line. "Now I know why so many of my girl secretaries have mysteriously disappeared!" she spat out. "You allowed the maniac upstairs to kill them—and then you disposed of their bodies in the courtyard well!" She looked at Marcia. "Now you can understand, my dear, why I locked you in your room tonight. I feared something like this!"

Tod Winston drew a sharp, agonized breath. He seemed about to say something; then evidently decided to keep his silence. It was as if he realized that any word of protest he might utter would bring a leaden slug smashing into his heart.

Grimly, the grey-haired Miss Gregory prodded him out of the room. "You follow us, Marcia, my dear!" she spoke over her shoulder.

Unsteadily, Marcia followed. Her fingers trembled as she tried to hold her thin, gossamer night-robe over her quivering breasts. The fragile garment had been ripped, torn in her struggles with Tod Winston, so that she was almost nude to the waist. Stumbling in the darkness, she followed Miss Gregory and the captive chauffeur down the winding stone steps.

They descended past the main floor, into the dank and fetid atmosphere of an underground cellar. A candle guttered weirdly on a stand. Miss Gregory shoved Tod Winston to a moss-damp, slime-slippery stone pillar beside the candle; tied him to the upright with a long length of heavy rope.

Then she stepped back, smiling grimly. "That will hold you until morning—until I can summon the police!" she remarked evenly.

Winston's eyes held a curiously-pleading quality as he stared at Marcia. Marcia turned away, shuddering. To think that she had allowed him to hold her in his arms, earlier that night; to… kiss her! And all the time he had planned to turn her over to the evil clutches of that foul, monstrous, misshapen madman in the barred cell at the top of the tower—

Miss Gregory touched Marcia's arm. "Come, my dear," she said gently. Marcia permitted herself to be led out of the underground dungeon, up the steps to her own little room. At the doorway, Miss Gregory smiled at her in the moonlight. "I will lock you in—as a matter of precaution," she said. "In the morning, when the police arrive and everything is safe, I'll release you."

Marcia hesitated. Then she stepped across the threshold. And at that instant, she heard Miss Gregory emit a gasping cry of warning. Marcia started to turn—

Something heavy thudded against her head, and everything went black. She sagged to the floor.

SHE opened her eyes, long moments later. She was on her bed. Spread-eagled. Her wrists roped over her head, her feet tied by the ankles to the bed-rails. She was helpless! And in the moonlight, she saw a man's form leaning over her—a man clad in chauffeur's livery!

"Oh, God!" she sobbed. Then Winston, the chauffeur, had managed to get loose! He had struck down Miss Gregory from behind; then had smashed something heavy against Marcia's skull, stunning her. And now he had tied her to the bed—

He leaned toward her, leering horribly. And then Marcia gasped out a choking cry. Because the man in chauffeur's livery was not Tod Winston! It was someone else—a stranger—someone she had never seen before!

In that instant, Marcia knew a sickening, nauseating fear. Blindingly, the real truth dawned on her dazed brain. The uniformed man whom she had seen carrying the red-haired girl's corpse, down in the castle courtyard—that hadn't been Tod Winston! It had been this other man—the one who bent over Marcia now! Tod Winston was guiltless!

He had come to Marcia's room, tried to rescue her from impending peril—and she had fought at him, screamed, caused him to be captured and tied up.... And now he was a prisoner in the dungeon below the castle, unable to help Marcia in her hour of need!

She stared into the leering, evil features of the man who loomed over her on the bed. She felt hard hands pawing at her breasts. She screamed.

The man chuckled demoniacally. "Go ahead!" he rasped. "Yell your pretty head off! It won't do you any good, little lady. I'm going to have my fun with you—and then I'll turn you over to the madman upstairs!"

Her captor's sinewy arms enfolded Marcia, smothered her. Sheer terror crawled and slithered through her veins, and icy horror congealed her spine. Wide-eyed, panting, struggling, helpless, she stared into the gleaming eyes of the man who held her. His face was utterly strange, yet somehow vaguely familiar.... And then, in a burst of recognition, Marcia knew the answer.

"Miss Gregory!" she shrieked the accusation.

AND the man who had masqueraded as a woman, who had posed as the grey-haired Miss Gregory, grinned savagely. "Smart girl!" he chuckled fiendishly. Then he pressed Marcia backward in the bed, kissed her savagely, brutally.

His hands were at her breasts, clawing, pawing; his slavering lips traversed her shoulders, the hollow of her throbbing throat. Sadistically he balled his fist, smashed a fury of savage blows at Marcia's hips, her thighs. He was ripping away the last remaining shreds of her gossamer night-robe from her cringing, tortured body....

From the doorway a gibbering snarl sliced the night. The man in livery stiffened, leaped to his feet, whirled. Marcia, staring, saw a grotesque, misshapen form lurching forward through the moon-light.

The madman!

The grey-haired man in livery staggered, recovered himself. A cry of fear issued from his flaccid lips. And then the insane monster hurled himself forward.

Marcia's reason tottered, swayed. Desperately she struggled against her fetters; but they held her implacably. She saw the hunchbacked maniac come to grips with his enemy; and she knew that if the madman triumphed, he would turn to her, bury his fang-like teeth in her throat, kill her... or worse....

To her mind there leaped a picture of what she had seen in the maniac's cell, earlier that night.... That was what would happen to Marcia—if the madman triumphed!

Then, numbly, she realized something else. Even if the man in chauffeur's livery killed the maniac, she still would die... horribly. Because the grey-haired, liveried man was also mad—utterly, demoniacally crazy! The sheer hellish horror of it battered at her consciousness. Two maniacs battling—with Marcia's body as the prize to the victor!

She twisted, squirmed. Her widened eyes watched the battle that raged all about the circular chamber. She saw the misshapen maniac's long, ape-like arms go out, crush his antagonist. She saw the hunchback's snake-like, writhing fingers close about the grey-haired man's throat. The grey-haired man gasped, choked, cried out horribly. He clawed and fought at the throttling fingers which were pressing out his life; but his struggles were in vain. Marcia heard the sickening snap of broken vertebrae; saw the liveried man's head loll sidewise horribly....

And then the misshapen one had flung his adversary's limp, dead body aside; had turned toward the bed. Now, leering, slavering from flaccid lips, uttering tiny cries of unspeakable triumph, he was slowly coming toward Marcia, with his murderous fingers out-thrust and writhing and twisting—

Marcia screamed; and her wailing cry held crystalline terror that verged on madness. The beast-man was nearly upon her now—

"*YOU* damned fiend from hell!" a voice suddenly roared from the doorway. And then a hurtling form catapulted into the room, smashed full into the maniac's misshapen back. The monster squealed like a trapped animal, tried to twist and writhe free. Marcia stared—and saw that the newcomer was Tod Winston!

Tod Winston, the chauffeur! And he was battering at the grotesque head of the maniac, smashing iron-hard, pistonlike blows to the madman's skull. The hunchback emitted a shrieking scream of fear; but Tod Winston knew no mercy for this killer-beast. He had the maniac down; was choking him, battering his head savagely against the floor.

And then, suddenly, it was over. The hunchback lay still; and from his split skull, blood and grey brains oozed thickly....

"Tod! Tod Winston!" Marcia gasped.

And then Winston was by her side, unfastening her fetters, freeing her. He was holding her in his arms. "My dear! My very dear!" he whispered.

"Tod—what happened? How did you get free?"

"I managed to reach that candle. Burned away the ropes at my wrists. I heard you screaming—and I ran up here. Thank God, I was in time!" he panted. He crushed her against him, held her tightly, so that her breasts were pressed thrillingly against his heaving chest.

"Tod—Tod!" Marcia whispered. "Did—did you know that Miss Gregory was… a man?"

"I suspected it. That's why I was here; that's why I had taken a job as chauffeur at Gregory Castle. You see, I'm not really a chauffeur."

"Not—not a chauffeur? Then—who are you?"

"Captain Tod Winston of the Army Intelligence Service," he answered slowly. "And that man who lies dead on the floor, killed by the hunchbacked maniac was… Colonel Lawrence Gregory! The man who built this castle, years ago!"

Marcia tensed. "But—that's impossible! Colonel Gregory died long years before this!"

"That's what he made people think. He had brooded because his bride deserted him, eloped with a lover. So he faked his own death; then assumed woman's attire and lived here under the pretense of being his own sister—a sister who never really existed."

"But—but how did you know? Why were you here?" Marcia gasped.

"Gregory was supposed to be buried at Arlington. The Government was sending his pension to his supposed 'sister.' Recently, some changes had to be made in the layout of the graves at Arlington. Colonel Gregory's body was to be moved to another location. The coffin was exhumed, opened as a matter of routine. Then it was discovered that a wax dummy had been buried in Gregory's stead. That's why I was sent here to investigate."

"*AND*— Colonel Gregory was alive… all the time?"

"Yes. Posing as 'Miss Gregory,' he lived here in the castle. And his warped brain conceived a fantastic scheme. He hated all women—because his own wife had deserted him. So he planned to revenge himself on the entire female sex. He lured young girls here, promising them secretarial work. Once they were in his power, he would… attack them. And then he'd turn them over to his pet madman, at the top of the castle tower. The madman would kill the girls… horribly. Then Gregory would lure a fresh victim… even as he lured you."

"And—and he put on a chauffeur's livery, just like yours, when he threw that girl's corpse down the well!" Marcia whispered.

Tod Winston nodded. "That was in case anyone was watching. It was his way of diverting suspicion—throwing it on me."

Marcia shuddered. "My dear—my dear!" she sobbed. "Will you ever forgive me for thinking that you… were the killer? Can you forgive me for not trusting you?"

He smiled gently. In the moonlight his face was softened, his eyes reverent. He touched Marcia's shoulders, her young breasts. Then he kissed her, gravely, on the mouth. "A man forgives everything in the woman he loves!" he whispered.

HUGH SPEER

ShE WhO WAS hE!

A strange story of a woman who knew the secrets of a man's honeymoon! And on that she based her claim that his wife was her bride!

I **HAVE twenty-four more** hours to live. Another night, and then a day and when tomorrow evening comes they will open my cell door and lead me out, a guard holding each arm, into the electrocution chamber.

I am alone in this portion of the grim-walled prison, for this is the death-cell in the women's wing, and I am a woman.

I set this down with all the bitter irony that is in my heart. I am a woman, I who was once a man. And they wouldn't listen to me. I forced my lawyer to call Doctor Klein's interne, and he told the court that I had been discharged as cured when I was hopelessly insane. But the court wouldn't believe him. And, of course, that was ridiculous.

So tomorrow I must die.

It is true there is the faint possibility of a commutation. The Governor withholds his decision until the last day, from a mistaken idea of mercy. But there is little chance of commutation for me.

Because, in spite of the interne, the experts found me sane. The prosecuting attorney told the jury that I was playing a clever racket. And, when I cried out in court that I was sane, they laughed, and the prosecutor complimented me. They said I was sane, and I am sane, but they wouldn't listen to what I had to say.

YOU'LL want to know why, if I really am Keith Bradford, I accepted the name of Mary Shane. That is the name that devil, Klein, gave me, when he dismissed me from his private sanitarium, a woman instead of a man. Oh, he was as shrewd and clever as they come. He'd even hired an old mother for me, in Kansas City, and witnesses who testified that they had known me in my girlhood. You see, Klein had stacked the cards pretty completely.

I thought, when I was discharged from the sanitarium, that Klein's motive had been a scientific one. I didn't dream that there was a deeper motive for his action.

I, Keith Bradford, was a prosperous young business man, and Molly and I had been married for three years. I admit that I was jealous of her. She was the daintiest and most ravishing creature that I had ever seen in my life.

Small, fair, vivacious, vivid, numbering her admirers by the score, accustomed to having every man she met fall at her feet and worship her. When I won her, I thought I was the luckiest man in the world. But, even after we were married, she couldn't resist having her little flirtations. I believe that they were innocent ones, as she always swore they were.

AFTER three years I fell sick. I suffered from violent headaches, and there were periods when everything seemed to fade out of my consciousness, and I didn't know where I was, or even who I was. We had a nurse at my home; then Dr. Klein diagnosed my case as that of a brain tumor, and he told Molly that I had one chance in three of recovering, if he operated—and none if he didn't.

That was how Klein got me to his Long Island sanitarium, and was able to accomplish his diabolical scheme.

I remember consenting to the operation, and seeing Molly's tearful face as I was taken away in the ambulance. I have a faint recollection, too, of the ether, and Klein standing by me, telling me to breathe deeply. His face was so grave and compassionate, how could I guess the devilish scheme that was fermenting in his mind?

IT was a long, long time afterward when I became conscious. And after that weeks went by, during which the sense of personality came back to me only by slow degrees. Yet the body healed much quicker than the mind, for I used to walk about the sani-

"You fiend!" I cried. "I'll kill you for what you've done to me."

tarium grounds with a nurse—I have some remembrance of that.

The final phase was instantaneous. One moment I was a dull-witted being, lying on the bed in the private room; the next everything had grown clear.

I remembered that I was Keith Bradford, that I had been sick for a long time, and had gone through a dangerous operation. But now I was myself again completely, with an extraordinary feeling of well-being.

And, now that I was well, I should soon be back with Molly. I couldn't conceal my impatience. I looked for a bell to ring, but there was none. I cried out for the nurse, but no one answered me. I tried to open the door and discovered that it was locked.

Some instinct made me look down at my legs and feet. To my astonishment, my feet seemed to have shrunk considerably. And they were encased in a woman's slippers. And on my legs were a

woman's black cotton stockings.

As I raised my hands, they struck my chest, and then a scream of horror broke from me. I had a woman's breasts, plump, well-developed, and bound with a gauzy brassiere!

I, Keith Bradford, who had gone into Klein's sanitarium a man, had somehow been turned into a woman!

FOR a few minutes I think I went mad. I raved and shouted, hammered upon the door and tried to break it down, but without success. Then I grew calm and sat down to consider the situation.

I had always been interested in medicine, and it wasn't difficult for me to come to a satisfactory conclusion about the matter. Klein, whom we had begun to know socially a short time before my operation, had spoken one night about the new extracts of the ductless glands, and the powerful part that they played in medical science.

He had spoken, in particular, of the new feminine sex hormone, that had been isolated in Germany, a substance so potent that no physician had dared explore its possibilities.

During my long mental illness he must have administered this fearful drug to me, or else implanted a fragment of glandular tissue somewhere in my body.

I saw a mirror hanging on the wall and looked at myself in it. I had always had a heavy beard, but there was now no trace of hair upon my face. The hair on my head, on the other hand, which had been coming out faster than I considered esthetic, at my age, had been replaced by a heavy, luxuriant crop, with a boyish bob.

The face that looked back at me was that of a woman of about eight and twenty, good-looking, and rather masculine. The features were those of Keith Bradford. But no one who had known me in the past could possibly have identified me with the husband of Molly Bradford.

I had just schooled myself to calmness when the lock turned, and Dr. Klein came in.

"Well, how are you today, Miss Shane?" he asked, and then started in astonishment at the evident change in me.

"Why—why, Miss Shane, I believe it's happened!" he exclaimed. "I knew that your memory would come back all at once. That's splendid, my dear girl. Just as soon as you've orientated yourself a little we shall be able to send you home."

"You damned devil!" I shouted. At least, I meant to shout, but the voice that came from my lips was a very feminine scream.

HE played his part to perfection, I must say that for him. He stepped back and surveyed me in simulated astonishment. His jaw sagged; he actually looked crestfallen.

I gave him no chance to keep up the pretense. "I came in here Keith Bradford, and you've changed me into a woman with your damned hormone!" I shouted. "Don't pretend you don't know all about it! I'll send you to the penitentiary for the rest of your life, unless—unless you change me back again," I ended weakly, conscious of the sob in my voice.

"Now, my dear girl, control yourself," he said when I paused for breath. His face had changed. Instead of the simulation of friendly interest, there was the professional mask.

"Try to think," he went on. "Don't you remember administering the ether to poor Keith when I operated on him last fall? Don't you remember how I got you out of a nasty jam with the hospital board, by telling them that his heart stopped owing to the incision in the brain, and not because of maladministration of the anesthetic?"

"So that's the line you're going to take, is it?" I stormed. "How do you think you're going to get away with that story, when Molly recognizes me? When I remind her of intimate things that have been between us in the past? Perhaps you mean to murder me?" I raved.

He withdrew so swiftly and silently that the door had clicked in my face before I could fling myself against it. I must have gone mad again, for I came back to consciousness to find a strong, grim-faced nurse gripping my arm, and the bedclothes strewing the room.

"Now, Miss Shane, that's enough of that," said my nurse, "or we'll have to put you in a strait-jacket. And that's not nice."

"But he's turned me into a woman," I sobbed hysterically. "Can't you see I—I'm different from when I came in? Oh, he couldn't have been clever enough to hide it from everybody in the sanitarium."

A young interne had come into the room, and was standing watching me. As I began to struggle again, he stepped forward, caught my arm, turned up my sleeve, and stuck a hypodermic needle into my arm.

I still fought madly for liberty, for in the depths of my mind was the idea that Dr. Klein meant to kill me, to hide the evidences of his crime. But in a minute or two I felt my strength relaxing and sleep overcoming me.

"She'll do now," I heard the young interne say. "The doctor's pretty well broken up about it. He was sure that she'd be her normal self when she regained full consciousness."

WHEN I awoke, the sunlight was streaming into my room.

The door was open, but I could hear voices in the corridor, and I knew that the nurse had only stepped outside for a moment. Thought of flight was futile. Besides, I was wearing a short woman's nightgown, of the kind given hospital patients, and my clothes were gone.

It seemed like a frightful dream to me, until I looked down and saw my breasts again, touched the soft fullness of their feminine curves, and knew for a surety that I was a woman.

And then, in an instant, the idea came to me. So long as I claimed to be Keith Bradford, Klein would have an excuse for keeping me in the sanitarium, keeping me away from Molly, and preventing me from taking measures for his arrest.

I must feign to believe that I really was Mary Shane. It wouldn't deceive Klein, but he couldn't hold me if I convinced all the staff that I was sane.

I was satisfied that neither the nurse nor the interne had the least suspicion of Klein's hellish work, though how and where he had performed it was, and still is, a mystery to me.

Accordingly, when the nurse came in, I greeted her cheerfully, and made no reference whatever to what had happened on the preceding day.

I could see the surprise in her eyes; I enjoyed the cautious way in which she tested my rationality, as she supposed she was doing.

In the middle of which, Klein and the young interne, Dr. Harris, walked into the room.

"Well, how's the patient, nurse?" asked Klein.

"I'm feeling better than I've felt for a long time," I answered. "Why, Dr. Klein, I—I didn't seem to recognize you for the moment! Everything seems so hazy since—since poor Mr. Bradford died, and they suspended me."

"Ah, so you remember that, Miss Shane, do you?" he answered guardedly. I could see he had guessed the purpose of my maneuver instantly, and he was casting about in his mind how to meet it.

"When did your memory come back to you, Miss Shane?" he asked me.

"I woke this morning feeling different somehow," I answered. "I've been sick a long time, haven't I? I'm looking forward to the time when I can go home."

"Well, we'll see about that," he answered.

In spite of my play, they watched me closely. It was not for several days that they trusted me to be alone without the nurse. But her, at least, I had convinced. From her I learned about the paralyzed old mother I was supposed to have in Kansas City, and other details of my past life, which I was able to put to good use.

I learned, in particular, that it was supposed to be the shock of my suspension, following Keith Bradford's alleged death on the operating table, that had resulted in my "mental breakdown."

Of course Klein, with his devilish cunning, had arranged to have an alleged Keith Bradford die under his knife, while I was being made the victim of his experiments.

Both the nurse and Dr. Harris had joined the staff subsequent to my advent, so of course they had no first-hand knowledge of the real Miss Shane, whoever she was.

IT was amusing, being a woman. I set to work to make a conquest of Dr. Harris, who was in his early twenties, an impressionable age. I would lie awake at night ransacking my brains and trying to remember the little tricks that women had used on me before I married Molly.

It amazed me, looking on men from the woman's point of view, and seeing how one could sway them.

"Oh, doctor, won't you help me roll these heavy stockings?" I asked the boy innocently one day. "Do you know, I've never worn anything but silk since I was a child?"

His face was red when he stood up. And I could see in his eyes that he no longer regarded me as a patient, but as a well woman.

"You're one of the prettiest girls we've had the good luck to have around here," he said, putting his arm around me, and then his hand reached for one of my breasts in a quick, eager caress.

I was amazed and horrified to find that I was conscious of something like a thrill, tingles of pleasure at the rough touch of his fingers on my skin.

*At first I hadn't
meant to kill them
both, but now...!*

"Now that's not nice, taking advantage of your patients that way, doctor," I answered lightly, slapping the offending hand.

He walked out as if treading on air. I could see he thought he had made a conquest. For a while I was afraid that the little episode would make him want to keep me longer in the sanitarium. And I was desperate for the feel of Molly's arms about me.

She'd be surprised, amazed, incredulous, when I explained to her who I was and what had happened to me, but, with her good sense and judgment, I felt sure that we should quickly be in a position to compel Klein to undo his vile work.

Klein by this time seemed to have accepted the situation. I didn't know, of course, that he had that paralyzed mother and the schoolgirl witnesses all hired, that he would have the amazing effrontery to go through with his knavish scheme. Nor had I any means of guessing that Klein had another motive than the advancement of pure science.

So the day came when I was discharged. I had carried on a lively flirtation with poor Harris, and the boy was deputized to see me aboard the train for Kansas City. Up to the last moment I kept up the pretense with Klein, as he with me. Not by the flicker of an eyelash did I betray myself when we said goodbye.

Poor little Dr. Harris was heartbroken when the train rolled out of the Pennsylvania Station, and he made me promise to write to him. Needless to say, I got off at the first stop in New Jersey and was back in New York by evening.

I had fifteen dollars in my purse, and by this time I was becoming accustomed to a woman's clothes. Eager as I was to see Molly, I resolved to wait till the morrow rather than agitate her so late at night, and accordingly I engaged a room at a hotel.

MY heart was beating fast when I approached our home in the pretty Long Island suburb. When Molly opened the door to me, I couldn't speak for a moment. I was disappointed to see that she was not in mourning—in gay colors, rather. But never had she looked so beautiful as when she stood there in front of me, looking at me as if I were a stranger.

"Why—why, it's Miss Shane!" she exclaimed suddenly. Evidently she hadn't heard of my illness as the supposed Miss Shane, for she went on:

"Please do come in, my dear. It's such a relief to see you. You got my letter, didn't you, in which I told you that I didn't hold you in any way responsible for poor Keith's death?"

As she spoke I felt a slight bitterness that Molly had failed to recognize me, and, mingled with it, a twinge of the old jealousy I had always had concerning her. I knew mourning was out of style, but need she have looked so very gay six months after my supposed burial?

Then and there the idea came to me to test her, to try out her loyalty to me before I revealed myself.

I let her talk, watching her the while. Her figure, always pretty, had grown more pronouncedly so, and her breasts, whose firm, round contours I had always loved so, were even fuller and more shapely, more enticingly feminine. I was surprised at first that I was less stirred by her physical charms than I had expected to be, till I remembered. For I was always on the point of forgetting that I was a woman.

"I'm glad you felt that way, Mrs. Bradford," I answered. "I'm sure you must miss your husband very much. Do you remember that night when you confessed you had been platonically attracted by another man, and said he was never to doubt you?"

"Why—why, Miss Shane!" she gasped.

"And those memories of your honeymoon trip," I went on. "When he asked you to make out a list of all your beaux, and you asked him if he didn't trust you!"

She had risen to her feet and was confronting me, fire in her eyes, and her beautiful bosom heaving. For a moment I was sure that she had penetrated my disguise, and was on the point of telling her all.

THEN I saw that even now, after what I had said, Molly didn't know me.

"Why—why, what do you mean by coming here and talking such intimacies to me?" she gasped.

"Look at me, Molly, and see if you don't recognize me," I answered, thinking again that the moment had come.

"I recognize you for the nurse who attended my husband here for three weeks before he went to the hospital," she answered. "But that gives you no right to call me anything but Mrs. Bradford, or to—to dare to speak of—what you've ventured to speak about. Good-afternoon!"

I chuckled at her words. Dear little Molly! But, as I was once more on the point of revealing myself, I heard a car draw up to the door, and saw, to my astonishment, Dr. Klein hurrying up to the house.

"I was passing and just had a moment, Molly—" he began, then ceased. "Why, what's the matter?" he asked.

"That woman," panted Molly, bursting into tears. "That nasty, snoopy nurse of poor Keith's, who's been retailing to me all the intimacies of our lives together, which I suppose she picked up from him when he was delirious!"

And she swung an accusing arm toward me as I stood in the entrance hall, smiling, for unexpectedly the chance had come to unmask Klein's villainy.

He saw me, and gave a great start of astonishment. "That woman is supposed to be on her way to Kansas City!" he cried. "She was discharged from the sanitarium yesterday morning, ostensibly cured. I doubt now whether she was cured at all. I didn't tell you, Molly, that she became insane and was in the sanitarium under treatment for six months."

"You liar!" I cried. "You damned, infernal liar! Molly, I'm Keith, your husband—Keith! He changed me into a woman while I was unconscious under drugs, by means of that damned sex hormone he used to talk about! Look at me, Molly, see if you don't recognize me! That's why I brought to your mind those intimate things of our life together."

And I advanced upon her with extended arms, ready to take her to my heart. But to my amazement she uttered a shriek and ran into Klein's.

And, as he stood there, with his arms about her, I saw from the possessive, caressing way in which his hands touched her breasts—saw from the whole demeanor of the man, that he was in love with her. And now at last I understood the hellish motive that had prompted him to destroy Keith Bradford and create me, the mythical Miss Shane.

"She's mad, Harry, she's mad! I'm afraid of her!" sobbed Molly. "Oh, do something! Get her out of this house and take her away, poor creature!"

THE COURIER

INSANE WOMAN AT LARGE IN CAR

POLICE WATCHING
ALL ROADS

NURSE DISCHARGED
FROM DR KLEIN'S SANI
TORIUM YESTER DAY
ASSAULTS WIFE OF
FORMER PATIENT

I laughed at the police;
I had but one object.

AT these words I recoiled—I had forgotten my woman's form and had been shaking my fist in Klein's face in my excitement. I drew back, crushed by the unexpected blow.

"Molly," I cried, "won't you just look at me? Aren't my features those of Keith Bradford's? Don't you remember when I bought you that little watch, and the day we took that excursion up the Hudson?"

I was sure she would know me then. Instead, she clung wildly to Klein, her arms about his neck.

"Take her away!" she sobbed hysterically. "She's mad, mad, dangerous! She's stored up everything that poor Keith must have talked about when he had those muttering spells. And she's come here to kill me!"

"Not you, but that arch-villain!" I screamed. "I'll fight you through every court in this land, Klein, even if my own wife doesn't recognize me now!"

I saw Klein glancing furtively about him. He was a little man, and, as Dr. Harris had told me, he used to carry a small blackjack in his pocket in case of attack by refractory patients. This was what he missed now, and he was afraid of me, woman though he had made me.

FOR an instant I was ready to beat him to a pulp, as I should have done in the old days. Then I realized that I must act prudently. I feinted at him, and then, as he drew back, and Molly screamed again, I dashed past him into the street. I had no mind to have him call the police and have me dragged back to the sanitarium.

I think he was too staggered to know just what to do for the moment. As I passed his car, I realized that the ignition was on, for the engine was turning over. Instantly I leaped inside and pressed down the accelerator.

Before Klein could reach the street, I was speeding toward open country.

INSANE WOMAN AT LARGE IN CAR
Nurse Discharged from Dr. Klein's Sanitarium Yesterday Assaults Wife of Former Patient and Steals Doctor's New Model Ford 8. Police Watching all Roads.

I laughed when I read the lying scare-head in a local paper, for by that time I was many miles away, and there were too many women driving cars of that make, for me to be in any danger of apprehension.

I came back along the Nassau Boulevard, where I knew the stream of traffic would preclude all possibility of my being stopped. For, as I have said repeatedly, by this time I had learned to act like a woman, and, in my quiet-colored, neat traveling suit, I certainly would not arouse the suspicions of any watching detectives.

If that newspaper had not stated that my house was being watched, if it had not added that Molly had gone to the sanitarium to recover from the nervous shock, I might have committed the folly of going home to plead with my wife once more. As it was, Klein had played into my hands.

*I stared at my reflection
in amazement. This
was not myself!*

For the sanitarium grounds were not patrolled at night, all the inmates being locked up by dark, and I knew a way up the rocky knoll on which the surrounding wall was built. And I knew a way over the wall. And I knew that Klein lived in a small cottage at one end of the grounds, with his housekeeper.

My plan was quickly made. I meant to confront him alone that night and force a written confession from him, under threat of immediate arrest. To assist me in carrying out this plan, I had the revolver with six loaded cylinders that I had found in a pocket of the car.

With Klein's written confession in my hands, I could easily convince Molly of the crime that had been committed, and give

Klein the alternative between restoring me to my male form and going to jail for life.

I PARKED the car some distance from the sanitarium, and started off afoot. The night was dark, the streets in that part of the town are dimly lighted, and soon I was at the base of the rocks.

A brief climb, and I was at the foot of the wall, and scrambling over at the place where some of the bricks had become dislodged.

I saw the two dark main buildings of the sanitarium, the administrative offices, in which a single electric light was burning, and the cottage at the end of the grounds.

There were lights in two of the rooms, and all the shades were drawn. It was a warm night, and the window in the front room was open. As the slight breeze stirred the shade, I saw the silhouettes of two figures outlined upon it, a man's and a woman's.

For a moment it didn't occur to me that the woman might be Molly. I didn't dream that Klein would have the hardihood to bring her there, with only the old housekeeper to play the role of chaperon.

Then, as the shade came to a rest for a moment, I saw the two heads close together, and realized that my wife was in Klein's arms.

I could hear their voices, and hers was cooing soft, as it had been when I was courting her.

"You've nothing to worry about, darling," Klein was saying. "The police are sure to have picked her up by morning, poor thing. Anyway, it's certain that she won't come here."

"I know, but I'm afraid, dear," Molly answered. "Do you know, there actually was a sort of resemblance between that woman and poor Keith. But what a mad idea, that she had been Keith! How did she get it?"

"Brooding over her suspension," answered Klein. "A conscientious woman, poor soul"—Oh, the lying dastard!—"but clever as sin. I admit she fooled me completely by pretending to have regained her sanity.

"Don't worry about her, darling. Think what a mercy it is that

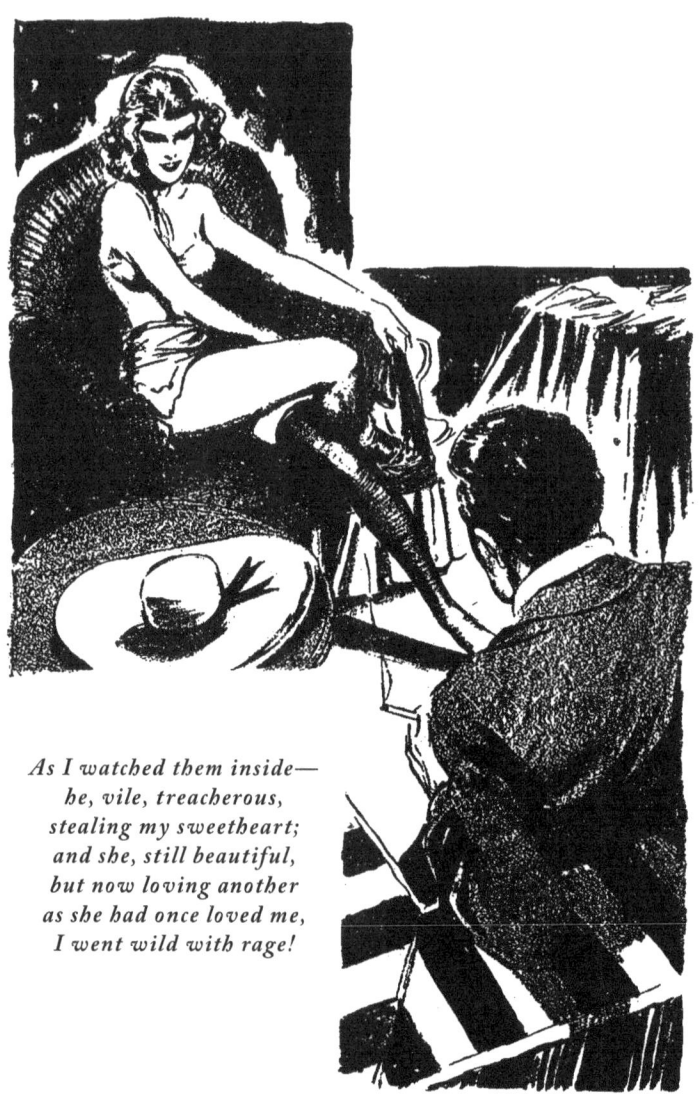

*As I watched them inside—
he, vile, treacherous,
stealing my sweetheart;
and she, still beautiful,
but now loving another
as she had once loved me,
I went wild with rage!*

poor Keith's dead. Otherwise he'd have found out sooner or later that we cared for each other."

"Poor Keith," sighed Molly. "He was a dear boy, but he hadn't a spark of romance, like you."

The heads changed position, and I heard the sound of a kiss, the short, gasping breaths of love's anticipation.

"And you won't insist on waiting any longer before becoming

my wife?" I heard Klein ask softly.

"I don't want to, darling," answered Molly.

I DON'T know how I had managed to endure the torture so long. Now a sudden blind fury seized me. I no longer thought of convincing Molly. Let her find out after Klein was dead. Yes, it was with full premeditation to kill that I leaped straight at the screen, wrenching it from the framework and carrying it with me into the lighted room.

Even so, I had forgotten that I was a woman and wore a woman's skirt. I tripped and fell headlong, but I still held the revolver fast.

Frantic with fear, Klein launched himself at me as I rose to my feet. I eluded him, and he went crashing into the wall. Molly, a look of horror on her face, was screaming at the top of her voice.

As I thrust the revolver into Klein's face, Molly leaped at me. I flung her off, and she fell headlong. I saw the knowledge of imminent death in Klein's eyes.

"I'm going to kill you," I said, "for stealing my wife's love, you rat. But, before I do, tell her that I'm Keith Bradford, whom you turned into a woman with your vile experiments."

"You're Keith Bradford—of course you're Keith Bradford," babbled Klein. "Don't shoot, for God's sake, Mary—"

I pressed the trigger, heard the roar of the discharge, saw Klein begin to lift his hands and then slump to the floor. Behind me, Molly was screaming like a demented woman, and there were yells outside

"Now you know! Now you know!" I cried to my wife. "You trickster, you false, lying trickster, I believe you knew me all the time!"

I might have spared her even then, but I couldn't bear the proud, defiant, fearless look upon her face: So I shot her three times through the breast.

THEN the door burst open, and two of the attendants and an office clerk came running in and seized me. My foot slipped in the pool of Molly's blood. I hadn't known that people had so much blood.

I am glad I killed her. She looked such a brave, pitiful little figure in death, the Molly who had once loved me. I am glad that I saved her from Klein's clutches.

I've told my story now, though nobody is likely to believe it, any more than they did in the court room. I wonder whether I shall feel any sensation when the current is turned on. I wonder how much of this woman's body of mine was once Keith Bradford's. I shall be glad to be free of it.

MARY SHANE'S SENTENCE COMMUTED

At the last hour, when the prisoner was actually being prepared to go to the chair, a phone message was received from Albany announcing that the Governor had decided to commute the death sentence on Mary Shane to imprisonment for life.

It is understood that the decision was the result of the reading by the medical officer of a rambling manuscript that the woman had been preparing for several days previously. This manuscript referred to an operation at some former date for a brain tumor.

An examination showed that the skull had been trepanned at some earlier time impossible to estimate, and therefore, acting upon medical advice, the Governor decided that the ends of justice would be served by the infliction of the lesser penalty.

ROBERT LESLIE BELLEM

LABYRINTH OF MONSTERS

*Never in the wildest nightmare of hell-
spawned horror could Travis imagine
such creatures as menaced the girl who
invaded his bungalow that night.*

*W*ITH *the coming* of midnight, a thick, glutinous fog had billowed in from the sea. Now the impenetrable grey pall settled silently over the little coast resort of Ghost Cove, blotting out the rows of summer cottages which clustered at the edge of the bay's whispering waters.

Wet mists collected on tree-limbs and cottage eaves; and droplets of moisture fell slowly, monotonously, like the *drip-drip-drip* of blood flowing from a hundred raw wounds. In the far distance, toward the frowning cliffs which imprisoned the cove, a loon shrilled eerily. Nearer, there came a faint shuffling sound in the sand, as of laggard footsteps dragging.

Within the bedroom of his rented duplex bungalow, Travis Brant stirred uneasily on his hard cot. He snapped on his flashlight, looked at the clock alongside his bed. Twenty minutes past midnight, the hands showed. Through an open window, curling tentacles of fog drifted into the room, like the ectoplasmic arms of a seeking, groping blind monster.

Brant arose to close the window. And as he thrust his feet into carpet-slippers, he stiffened. *What in God's name was that?*

IT came again, a weird, wailing cry that stabbed through the night's ghostly mist. Ululant with terror, laden with dread, it seemed to come from the other half of the duplex bungalow. Soul-chilling, spine-curdling, the scream rang out still a third time.

With a curse, Travis Brant hurled his two hundred pounds of

brawny body toward his front door; smashed out into the engulf-
ing fog. A gust of salt-tanged breeze brushed his cheek like the
touch of ghost-fingers; and the fog-mists eddied and parted for
a brief moment.

Brant stared downward at the floor of the small porch on which
he stood. And then he drew a great, gulping breath; and icy talons
of nameless dread clutched deep into his heart. The porch was
wet and glistening with spilled, crimson blood!

Even as Travis Brant's eyes widened, he heard again that weird
and horrifying scream. This time there was no mistaking its source.
The sound came from the other half of Brant's duplex.

Snatching up a dressing-gown Brant lunged toward the door
from which that wailing cry had gibbered into the night. He saw
that the portal was open; saw a faint light within. He hurled
himself inside the place.

And as he crossed the threshold he plummeted into a soft and

With all his strength he heaved the pitcher at the little monster's head.

yielding form, a warm, trembling body that suddenly clung to him in sheer, crystalline terror.

"What the hell!" Travis Brant gritted; and then he swung the beam of his flashlight full upon the form that had clutched at him. He drew a sharp breath of amazement and stupefied admiration.

It was a girl, a young, brown-haired girl of breath-taking beauty. She was clad in shimmering, diaphanous pajamas, and there was a splotch of blood on her bare, lovely shoulder. Her brown eyes were wide, staring, filled with the slithering seeds of fear-madness. Her crimson, kissable lips were parted, contorted.

Through the gauzy thinness of the pajamas, Travis Brant could see the girl's heaving, panting breasts, twin ripe half-melons of cream-white flesh that strained at the pajama jacket like swelling mounds of enchantment. Her hips were lush, feminine, rounded; and her entire body was filled with a terror-trembling that was not pleasant to behold.

Even as Travis Brant stared at her, the brown-haired girl flung herself upon him once more. Her arms went about his neck, and her fragrant, feminine body blended and merged with his own, as if she sought to fuse herself upon him and to hide herself in his protecting masculinity.

SOMETHING of the girl's icy terror seemed to leap from her veins and enter Travis Brant's blood like a frigid rip-tide. And then, from somewhere in the house behind her, Brant heard a slithering, susurrant whisper of sound, as though a scuttling *thing* were moving across the floor.

"Oh, God!" the brown-haired girl gulped spasmodically, as a paroxysm of fear throbbed through her. "Take me away—before it grabs me and… tears out my throat… *the way it tore out that other girl's throat!*"

"Good Lord!" Travis Brant grated. "What are you talking about?" His arms enfolded the brown-haired girl. He shook her, trying to restore sanity to her staring eyes. "Who are you? What's it all about?" he rasped.

"I—my name's Anne Barnard. I live here in this half of the duplex. I j-just moved in this afternoon…."

"Yes. Go on!"

"A while ago, I—I was asleep. Something awakened me. Footsteps outside…. Then my front door opened. Somebody staggered into my bedroom. It was a girl, a Chinese girl. She was naked… and bleeding from a raw wound in her throat."

"That accounts for the blood I saw here on the porch!" Travis Brant clipped out.

"Yes! I—I switched on my lights, stared at the Chinese girl. There… there was *something*… clinging to her breast. At first I thought it was an infant. And then—and then I saw…" Anne Barnard's voice quivering and gurgled into a low-pitched moan of sheer horror.

"Go on! You saw what?" Travis Brant whispered.

"The—the *thing* at the Chinese girl's breast was not an infant. It was… something else. Something foul—horrible—impossible! Its talons were fastened in her b-breasts; its fangs were at her throat. It was *drinking her blood!*"

"God!" Travis Brant rasped. "What was it? What was the thing?"

"I—I don't know!" the brown-haired Anne Barnard wailed shrilly. "It was horribly hairy… all over! It was tiny, and white… and its face was dripping with the Chinese girl's blood! It had no legs—*and four long arms!*"

Travis Brant stared at the girl. Was she mad? Was she suffering from the delusions of insanity? Then he noticed her blood-stained shoulder. He touched it. "This—?" he whispered.

"I—I tried to tear the *thing* loose from the naked Chinese girl. It snarled at me, clutched me with one of its four hands. Its claws scratched my flesh! I screamed and ran out of the house. Then I bumped into you!" Abruptly, Anne Barnard went limp; collapsed utterly.

TRAVIS BRANT caught her as she slumped. Caught her, lifted her, carried her into his own half of the duplex. He laid her on his own bed; stared down at her for a single instant. His eyes took in the swelling glories of her firm breasts through her thin pajama-coat; swept over the lilting contours of her torso, her hips, her thighs. Then he whirled and dashed back out into the fog.

He reached the open front door of the adjoining half of his duplex cottage, the half occupied by Anne Barnard. He plunged inside. And as he passed the portal, it seemed as though slimy tentacles of oozing dread reached into his soul with questing, cold, gelatinous fingers. For a single instant he hesitated, and salt sweat dribbled from his forehead into his eyes, his mouth. Then he squared his shoulders; forced himself forward.

He reached Anne Barnard's bedroom. His eyes went wide, and he felt the blood draining from his strained features. "My God!" he cried wildly, savagely. "My God!"

Thick nausea nibbled at his churning belly. He felt sickening revulsion sweeping over him like a black tidal wave. His eyes were riveted as though hypnotically magnetized, upon a sprawled, outstretched form on the floor at his feet….

The dead body of a naked woman, a girl. A dark-haired Asiatic girl, slant-eyed, lovely, young and yet thick with maturity. Her heavy, swelling breasts were bruised and lacerated; her almond eyes were wide, glazing, sightless. Her throat was a ripped and bleeding wound—a great, gory gash from which the crimson had spewed in a thick freshet, running down over her breasts, her rounded ivory body.

And then, from the shadows of a far corner, Travis Brant heard a sudden, mewling, threadlike wail—a tiny cry of utter, demoniac, nameless evil. It was as though a damned soul had spoken from the slimy slopes of hell itself!

Travis Brant's gaze went toward that sound. And then he felt his knees going weak, and a chill terror gripping his intestines. Something was moving toward him, moving crablike across the floor, horribly, obscenely.

NEVER in the wildest nightmares of hell-ridden, fiend-spawned horror could such a creature be envisioned. Its tiny white-ivory body was covered with fine, thin black hair through which the flesh showed with scaly luster. It had no legs; but from its shoulders grew four long, flaccid arms, many-jointed and snake-like.

All four arms ended in clawing, long-nailed caricatures of human hands. The creature's face was a Godless obscenity. It had no eyes, no ears; and where its nose should have been, there were two distended, bloody holes. Its mouth was a slavering red slash that ran from cheek to cheek, and from the curled-back lips, sharp jagged fangs protruded redly. And yet, despite the unutterable, fantastic hideousness of that face, there was some faint quality of humanness about it—as though the thing were a blasphemous travesty of a human infant, fashioned by a sadistic Satan in the foulest reaches of hell.

It was moving toward Travis Brant, pulling itself blindly with its four groping, tentacle-like arms. And as it moved, there issued from its mouth a series of those thin, thread-like mewling cries, blood-hungry and horrible.

Suddenly it reached the Chinese girl's body. Like a flash, it battened itself upon the corpse's breasts, clinging with all four clawing hands, the sharp nails digging demoniacally into dead, pliant flesh.... Its fanged slash of a mouth fastened on the girl's gory, torn throat. Then, while Travis Brant watched in nauseated fascination, it began to suck the dead woman's clotting, congealing blood.

Abruptly, the thralls of Travis Brant's icy paralysis were broken. With a wild oath, he leaped forward, picked up a heavy pitcher from the wash-stand, hurled it with all his strength full at the tiny monster's blood-battening head. The pitcher smashed into crimson-dripping shards against that evil little skull.

There came the sound like the splitting of a ripe cocoanut, and the miniature hell-beast sprawled lifelessly backward, kicking and squirming spasmodically in the throes of its death-agony. Its brains made a spewing grey ooze on the rug... then, slowly, it stiffened and grew still.

Sobbing in his constricted throat, Travis Brant turned and raced out of the room, out of the house, into the spectral-damp fog outside. He plunged into his own half of the duplex cottage, hurtled into his bedroom.

THE brown-haired Anne Barnard was sitting up in the bed. Her hand was pressed over her left breast, as if to still the wild, insane thrumming of her heart. "You—you saw the *thing?*" she whispered.

"Yes!" Travis Brant muttered thickly. "I saw it! And we've got to get the police—right away!"

Abruptly the girl sprang from the cot. She threw herself at Brant; clung to him hotly, thrillingly, frantically. "You—you can't leave me here!" she panted.

"Then come along!" he grated grimly. His arm encircled her lithe waist; and as if magnetized, his hand drew upward toward the swelling base of her breast. His fingers pressed into that firm, rounded mound. Together, they raced from the cottage, into the fog-bound night.

Ahead of them, two blobs of yellow light suddenly loomed

The iron spike split through the bone as if it had been tissue paper; pierced the brain.

through the glutinous grey mist. An automobile's headlights! Travis Brant sprang toward the machine—and as he drew near it, he gulped a great, gasping breath of sheer relief. It was the official police car of Ghost Cove—and Patrolman Dennis Mahony was at the wheel!

MAHONY was a big, raw-boned Irishman, an intrepid, steady-eyed man with whom Travis Brant had got fairly well acquainted during the past few weeks. They'd fished together in the Cove, two or three times; had played a little poker in the town's tiny jail-building. Now Travis Brant sprang on the policeman's running-board.

"Mahony—for the love of God, man!" he rasped. "Come with me quick! There's been a murder!"

The officer's eyes narrowed. "Murder, ye say?" he barked. He leaped from his machine. "Where? Where's the body?"

Travis Brant clutched Mahony's arm, dragged him back toward the duplex cottage. Anne Barnard followed fearfully. Mahony's service .38 was in his steady fist as they entered the front doorway of Anne Barnard's portion of the duplex.

Into the dimly-lighted bedroom they swept. "Look!" Travis Brant whispered. He pointed to the corpse of the mutilated Chinese girl. And then he went white.

The carcass of that blood-drinking little monster—the bestial and tiny thing of evil which Brant had slain with the water-pitcher—was gone! The bloody little dead thing had vanished, utterly and completely!

"Who was this dame? What killed her?" Mahony, the police-man, muttered thickly.

"I don't know who she was!" Travis Brant rapped out. "But I know what killed her. It was a small, foul, beastlike monster that ripped out her throat. I saw it—I killed it—and now it's disappeared!"

Mahony stared at Brant, as though he entertained doubts as to the man's sanity. And then Anne Barnard choked out a frightened, gasping whisper. "When—when the Chinese girl came into my bedroom, she gurgled something about Dr. Zenarro having killed her."

"Dr. Zenarro, is it?" Patrolman Dennis Mahony grunted. "I know the buzzard! He lives in that big, spooky house by the cliffs. They do say he deals with banshees and omadhauns! We'll go and question that laddy-buck right now!"

As he spoke, the officer picked up the Chinese girl's blood-stained cadaver, slung it over his shoulder.

And as he carried his gruesome burden toward the front door, he looked at Anne Barnard. "I'll be wanting you to come along, miss," he said grimly. "I'll be wanting you to tell about this dame's accusation, right to Dr. Zenarro's ugly mug!"

The brown-haired girl shrank backward. "You—you want me to go to that gloomy house of Dr. Zenarro? I—I'm afraid!"

Then Travis Brant slipped a hard arm about Anne Barnard's warm, thrillingly-feminine waist. "It's all right!" he whispered. "I'm going along with you!"

SHE cast him a frightful, grateful glance; and there was something in the passionate depths of her lovely eyes that filled Brant with leaping tingles of desire, of anticipation.

Out in the swirling, thickening fog, Dennis Mahony stuffed the corpse of the Asiatic girl in the back of his sedan. Then he slid under his steering-wheel; and Anne Barnard and Travis Brant got in beside him. The machine moved slowly, ominously through the wraith-tentacles of fog.

Ten minutes later they drew up before a vast, rambling black house set midway up the high and frowning cliffs overlooking Ghost Cove. The place was a somber, spectral structure of slimy grey stone, wet and viscid in the dripping night.

Brant and Anne Barnard followed the bulky figure of Patrolman Mahony as he stepped up to the porch of the house. And as the officer raised his huge fist and knocked thunderously on the heavy oaken door, Travis Brant felt a cold premonition creeping through his veins, like the oozing of some primordial fear.

He held Anne Barnard closer to him; and the warmth-fragrance of her tender body was like a bulwark to which he fastened his sanity and his courage.

A long moment they waited, in that fog-shrouded night of unreality and nightmare-horror. And then footsteps resounded hollowly within the house of Dr. Zenarro, like the echoing dim treads of doom. The heavy door swung open.

Travis Brant tensed.

The man who had opened the door was a huge, ungainly, shuffling creature clad in butler's livery. But there was something bestial and obscene about the fellow—a weird, chilling aura of utter evil. The man's long arms hung almost beyond his knees, and his head was sunk low between his broad, sloping shoulders. Hairy, his hands were, and his face was a thing of stark malignance.

Fang-like teeth jutted from between slavering, drooling lips; the eyes were oddly narrow, eerily gleaming with some demoniac and hell-born inward glow.

Patrolman Dennis Mahony spoke sharply. "I want to see your master, Dr. Zenarro. Take me to him."

"Yes," the liveried servant growled deep in his barrel-chest. "I am Gorill, and I will take you to him. You will come inside." There was something in the servant's voice that prickled the short red hairs at the nape of Travis Brant's neck. A sudden desire flamed in Brant's brain—a seething impulse to leap forward and smash his hammer-like fists into the butler's leering, evil features.

But he restrained himself. He followed Patrolman Mahony into the dark, dank house; and Anne Barnard clung to his arm, trembling strangely. The butler led them into a tiny ante-room, lighted a small electric lamp. "You will wait here!" he snarled.

Dennis Mahony shook his head grimly, "No. I'll follow you. You'll take me to Dr. Zenarro. My friends, here, will wait in this room for me."

Silently the servant nodded; but there was a sardonic, saturnine flare in his yellow-gleaming eyes.

He led the police-officer out of the little ante-room; closed the door. And now Travis Brant was alone with Anne Barnard.

She turned to Brant, crept toward him. "I—I'm afraid in this place!" she whispered falteringly. "There's something evil, horrible, about it… like the odor of a tomb!"

Brant drew her toward him. "It's all right!" he told her gently. "I'll take care of you." Then, on impulse, he tilted her tremulous chin, lowered his mouth to her parted lips.

She returned his kiss, ardently, warmly, thrillingly. Brant felt the fluttering tip of her moist little tongue, and lancing shivers of desire coursed through him. His hand crept to the front of her pajama-jacket, unfastened it, explored tentatively within the silken-gauzy garment. She pressed her body closer to his.

AND then, suddenly, Brant heard a faint, hissing sound. *"What's that?"* he gasped. He disengaged Anne's arms from about his neck; turned swiftly, seeking the source of that susurrant sound. At the

The masked man brought down the whip-lash again and again. Welts appeared on the girl's flesh.

same instant, he felt an abrupt choking sensation in his throat, and the blood began to pound strangely in his ears, his temples.

He looked at Anne Barnard. She had gone corpse-pale; was swaying toward him. Her breath was coming in sobbing gasps. "I—I can't breathe!" she whimpered. "Something's choking me!"

And it was choking, strangling, Travis Brant at the same time. An acrid, reeking agony was throttling the breath in his lungs, his throat. He whirled, hurled himself at the ante-room's closed door.

"God in Heaven!" he rasped. "It's locked! *We're prisoners!*"

And then he realized that the room was air-tight, hermetically-sealed, and that through some secret vent, an anaesthetizing gas was being introduced into the chamber! A gas that was robbing him of his senses, his consciousness.

Again he smashed against the locked door. It repulsed him. He felt himself swaying, toppling, falling. Anne Barnard had already slumped to the floor. Now he joined her, and the roaring in his ears became a hellish horror of sound which ended in nothingness.

When he opened his eyes, he was in a moisture-dripping subterranean passageway, dank and humid and filled with a smothering necrotic odor, the odor of decayed bodies, of long-dead, putrescent flesh. Someone was shaking him savagely, trying to arouse him.

He looked up—and stared into the fiend-gleaming eyes of a tall, broad-shouldered man clad entirely in black—clad in hell-black tights, black mask, black skull-cap. Through slits in the mask, the man's eyes glowed redly, Satanically.

"Come, come, my snooping friend!" the black-clad man growled evilly. "Get up! You are going on a nice journey through my labyrinth of caves!"

Dim electric lights glowed in the earthen walls of the underground passage, and seeping wetness stained the jutting rocks. From somewhere far along the tunnel, Travis Brant heard a series of mewling wails, foul and demoniac. Where had he heard such weird, eerie sounds before? And then he remembered. That tiny, furry creature which had battened on the Asiatic girl's life-blood—it had emitted exactly the same wailing cries!

Brant staggered to his feet; saw a snub-nosed automatic in the steady hand of the black-clad, demoniac man who was his captor. From the man's black mask came a rasping, guttural, snarling laugh. "I will let you sample the hospitality of Dr. Zenarro!" he chuckled softly, ominously.

"You—you are Zenarro?"

"Aye. I'm Zenarro, my friend. As you will learn to your sorrow!" The black-clad, mysterious one prodded Brant with the automatic. "Get going!"

AS Travis Brant stumbled forward, he beheld a cringing, fettered feminine figure before him. "Anne! Anne! Barnard!" he choked.

The brown-haired girl turned frightened, pleading eyes toward him. Her pajamas had been ripped from her lovely body, until only a thin gauzy shred remained about her middle. Her figure was hauntingly beautiful, a symphony in white girl-flesh. Her tapered legs melted fluidly into the columns of her creamy thighs; her lithe waist swelled upward toward the prominences of her alluring young breasts. There was horror in the tremulous twist of her red lips, and in the slithering fear that dwelt in her eyes. "Travis!" she whimpered.

"Move on!" the black-clad, demon-like Dr. Zenarro rasped. "There is no time to be wasted!"

For an instant, Travis Brant contemplated the thought of flinging himself at Zenarro; facing that automatic, chancing death, gambling against impossible odds. It was as if Zenarro had read his thoughts, for the man's finger squeezed on the trigger. The weapon belched flame, vomited a bullet past Travis Brant's head. "The next one will not miss, my friend!" the doctor whispered silkily.

Brant's shoulders sagged. Dully, he realized that he stood no chance in combat with Zenarro, as long as the man held that automatic. He must wait until Zenarro was off-guard.

Now they were shambling along that subterranean passageway. They rounded a bend. Far below, Travis Brant heard the whispering murmur of the surf, and knew that this cave must be in the cliffs behind Zenarro's house above Ghost Cove. Propped in an angle of the earthen corridor, Brant suddenly perceived a slumped figure—recognized it.

It was the body of Patrolman Dennis Mahony, clad in his olive-drab uniform, trussed, helpless, motionless, white-faced!

Brant's heart sank. No use looking for help from Mahony, now! Stiffly the officer lay there in that underground niche, as though deep in unconsciousness.

And then, abruptly, Dr. Zenarro prodded his two prisoners into a great cavernlike chamber, lighted with weird bluish effulgence from two semi-concealed, ghost-sputtering Cooper-

Hewitt lamps. But it was not the evil blue glow that brought a choking sob of horror to Travis Brant's dry throat. It was something else.

His eyes widened. What hellish nightmare was this? The place was lined with barred cages, and with medieval-looking instruments of torture. There was a rack, and there were branding-irons, and sharp-spiked torture-tables.

BUT the cages! God above! Travis Brant felt his stomach churning to a black froth of despair. In each of the iron-barred apertures there was a half-naked woman! There were white women, and negresses, and Japs and Chinese and Filipinos. And each creature held infantile forms—monster-nightmares of unutterable foulness!

One girl's arms cradled a malignant, two-headed creature—a tiny *thing* with one body and two heads, so that each of its twin mouths nuzzled at the woman's two white breasts. The dull gleam of stark insanity was in the mother's lack-luster eyes, and she rocked the evil little monstrous infant with solicitous maternal affection.

In another cage, a black woman gibbered and crooned over a hairy, miniature shape that had five legs and no arms, no eyes, almost no head. In still another, a brown-skinned Malay girl tended the wants of a hell-spawned *thing* whose arms grew out of its thighs, and whose mouth was located foully in the center of its forehead.

The black-clad Zenarro chuckled fiendishly. "Quite a collection, eh, my friend?" he whispered. "And they all belong to me! Soon I will sell these freak-monsters to European circuses, for much money! And then I will raise a new herd to replace them."

"You beast out of hell!" Travis Brant rasped unsteadily. "You—you father of monsters!"

"But no!" Zenarro corrected softly. "I am not the father. I am merely what, in show parlance, you might call the *entrepreneur*. I raise these creatures for profit. But the father is my huge and shambling servant, the man Gorill, who admitted you to my house."

She clung to him in sheer, crystalline terror.

"You—you mean—?"

"I will explain, since you seem interested. You may recall the case of a fellow named Modescu, a Rumanian miner in the Pennsylvania coal fields. The newspapers gave it much publicity at the time. This Modescu's wife gave birth to a monster infant—a nightmare horror, abominably deformed. Modescu went mad; killed his wife and the newborn child. He was incarcerated in an asylum—but later he escaped. Well, my friend, that same Modescu is none other than my servant, whom I have re-named Gorill—after the gorilla, you understand."

TRAVIS BRANT stared at the black-masked, black-clad Dr. Zenarro. Understanding was beginning to dawn in Brant's reeling brain, and his marrow crawled as though filled with maggots of madness.

Zenarro went on calmly. "This servant of mine has an unfortunate glandular affliction which causes all his offspring to be monsters. I rescued him from his pursuers and brought him here. And now he serves me well. I make much money from his… er, glandular peculiarity. I bring women here, force them to mate with Gorill. They bear monster-children, whom I sell to European circuses. A very profitable enterprise.

"Unfortunately, there is occasionally born a monster more savage than the rest—one which perhaps demands living blood instead of mother's milk. Such was the case of that Chinese girl who escaped from here tonight."

"God!" Brant gasped thickly. "That—that crab-like *thing* was her own child?"

"Yes. And it killed her, clung to her as she escaped. She could not free herself of it. It tore out her throat. I am sorry you killed that little monstrosity, my friend. I could have got a good price for it. However, I will breed another to replace it. In fact, this girl who came here with you tonight shall be mother to a new monster!"

Anne Barnard suddenly went white. She raised her fettered hands to her mouth; tried to run, to dart out of this chamber of foul horror. But Zenarro tripped her, and she went sprawling. At the same instant, Travis Brant lunged at the black-clad fiend.

But Zenarro was even swifter. He raised the muzzle of his automatic, smashed it down on Brant's unprotected skull. Blinding facets of light crashed across Brant's eyes, and he sagged into semi-stupor, with a constellation of agony stabbing at his brain.

Dimly he perceived the huge, ungainly, ape-like form of the liveried butler coming forward, lifting him, carrying him to a wall of the chamber. He felt iron rings being clamped about his wrists; the rings attached to a clanking chain; the chain drawn through a huge spike jutting from the wall. He sagged limply against his iron bonds.

THROUGH blurred eyes, he saw Zenarro bend forward, lift Anne Barnard to her feet. The black-clad doctor pawed at her quivering breasts. Then Zenarro's guttural voice drifted to Travis Brant's pain-dulled ears. The doctor was addressing Anne Barnard—

"You will be Gorill's mate, my dear. He will be the father of your child. Will you go to his arms willingly?"

"Never!" the girl wailed. "I'll die first!"

"No! But you will suffer much... until you either go mad, or accept Gorill's caresses!" Swiftly, savagely, Zenarro thrust the almost-nude brown-haired girl against a wooden cruciform frame; strapped her wrists to the cross-member, spread-eagled her ankles, tied them tight to the lower part of the framework. Pinioned, pilloried, she was held there by her bonds. Her eyes were wide with horror.

Zenarro picked up a long whip-lash. "Now!" he grated. He raised the quirt, brought it singing, stinging down across Anne Barnard's cringing body. Great, red welts appeared on her white flesh, like living serpents under her milky skin. Again and again Zenarro lashed at her, savagely, horribly.

And then the girl sagged. Her head lolled, and her eyes closed in the merciful oblivion of unconsciousness.

Zenarro spat disgustedly through a slit in his mask. "Pfah! She has fainted!" He turned to his hulking servant. "I am going back to the house, Gorill. Watch the girl—and when she regains her senses, signal me. You understand?"

The shambling, ape-like man nodded. Then Zenarro turned and left the cavern.

In the far corner, Travis Brant's numbed, pain-dulled senses were gradually clearing. His mind was beginning to function once more. He saw the gorilla-like servant approaching Anne Barnard's bound, unconscious form. The man was untying, untrussing Anne's limp arms and ankles. "I will carry you to the mating-chamber!" Gorill was muttering. "I will revive you with my kisses; and then we will make love... much love! We do not need Dr. Zenarro to watch!"

And then the ape-like brute lifted Anne, cradled her in his huge arms, carried her out of the cavern!

STRENGTH seeped back into Travis Brant's sinews. Cold horror was on him, and a dread chill, a savage red rage. Anne Barnard—sweet, innocent—at the mercy of that foul beast-man! It was too much for sanity to contemplate. Brant gathered his muscles, gained his feet, plunged against the chains that held him.

Again, again, again, he plummeted forward. And then, suddenly, he went sprawling. That iron spike had pulled out from the wall!

He was free!

Like a flash, he gathered up the long length of chain. His wrists were still bound together by those iron bracelet-rings; but he was otherwise untrammeled! He bounded out of the cavern. He must find Patrolman Dennis Mahony; and together, the two of them would rescue Anne Barnard—

Brant was in the subterranean passageway now. He came to the niche where Mahony lay stiffly, lifelessly. He bent down over the policeman.

"God!" he rasped in his throat as his fingers recoiled from those cold, waxen features. Brant straightened, whirled, hurled himself back along the passageway. He passed the cavern of cages, the cave of monsters and mad, insane, mindless, unwilling mothers… Then, at last, he reached another, smaller chamber in the earth.

Within that chamber, the ape-like servant was forcing Anne Barnard toward a cot. The girl had recovered consciousness, and she was fighting with all her vain, useless strength. Gorill was bending her backward….

With a mighty, snarling oath, Travis Brant leaped into that foul place. In his iron-bound hands he grasped the spike which he had pulled from the wall. He raised it high—brought it plunging down into the liveried servant's skull. The iron spike split through bone as though it had been tissue-paper; pierced Gorill's brain. The servant slumped lifelessly to the earthen floor, limp, dead.

Travis Brant sprang at Anne Barnard, swept her into his arms. And at that instant, a harsh voice floated through the labyrinth of caverns. Dr. Zenarro's voice. "Gorill—where are you? What have you done with that girl? Gorill—Gorill!"

The voice was coming closer now. Travis Brant's face was white, grim, set. "Listen, Anne darling!" he whispered. "This is our only chance of overcoming that mad doctor. Are you willing?" And he whispered something into the girl's ear.

She clung to him, pressed her body close to his own. "Y-yes!" she answered faintly.

And then Travis Brant sprang at the liveried, dead servant; stripped the corpse of its butler's garb. He drew the trousers on over his own pajamas; and since he could not don the coat because his wrists were fettered by the iron chains, he merely placed the livery over his shoulders like a cape. Then, in the semi-darkness, he pressed Anne Barnard back toward the cot....

She moaned with fright, with pain. Brant's mouth was pressed upon her lips, and his chained hands touched her breasts, fondled those swelling mounds of enticement. Darting thrills ran through his veins at the intimate contact with her body....

And then Brant stiffened. Footsteps had stopped directly outside the chamber. He heard Zenarro's chuckling, evil voice. "So you decided to mate with her before I got back, eh, Gorill?" the man rasped.

ZENARRO entered the little cave; came close to the cot. And as he leaned forward, unsuspecting, Travis Brant hurled himself upright, gathered his muscles, sprang—full at the black-masked doctor's throat.

Cat-like, Zenarro leaped backward. His eyes widened behind his mask as he perceived that the man in livery was not his servant, but was his supposed prisoner, Travis Brant, the man he intended to kill. Zenarro's hand whipped up. It held the automatic. He fingered the trigger spasmodically.

Flame roared from the gun's muzzle, and Travis Brant felt a scalding slug tear into his shoulder. But no bullet could stop Brant's mighty leap. He smashed himself full at his enemy, raised his blood-stained iron spike, drove it home in Zenarro's heart.

Zenarro collapsed, coughing bloody, crimson-frothed spew from behind his mask. He twisted, writhed—and suddenly became very still, with the stillness of sudden death.

Travis Brant lurched toward the prone body. "You know who this man was?" he whispered harshly to Anne Barnard.

"N-no. Who?"

"A man nobody would ever have suspected. I myself would never have guessed, except that I tried to arouse that unconscious figure of our friend Patrolman Dennis Mahony, out in the passageway. And when I tried to arouse him, I discovered—*that it was a wax figure! A dummy placed there to fool anyone who might stumble upon it!*"

"You mean—?"

"I mean that Dennis Mahony was a policeman part of the time; and the rest of the time he was Dr. Zenarro!" Travis Brant gritted. He whipped away the mask from the dead man's features, and disclosed the face of Mahony, the Irish cop! "That accounts for the disappearance of the little monster that killed the Chinese girl!" Brant breathed harshly. "He was right there on the scene all the time, probably looking for his escaped victim. While I was in my bedroom with you, he was in your half of the duplex, making away with the corpse of the monster. He had time to get back to his sedan before you and I ran out into the fog and came upon him!"

Anne Barnard crept close to Brant. "W-what is to be done now?" she whispered.

"We'll get out of here, notify the authorities. Those poor caged, insane women will be sent to some asylum. Their monster-children will be mercifully destroyed. And meanwhile, you and I—"

"Y-yes, Travis Brant? What about you and me?"

Brant caught her with his iron-gyved hands. "We'll find a minister who'll marry us!" he answered softly, gently.

She smiled at him; pressed herself thrillingly against him. And then, together, they wended their way upward out of that cavern-labyrinth of horror. And when at last they reached the open, they saw that the fog had dispersed, and the stars were very bright.

ROBERT LESLIE BELLEM

TAUPOO DANCE

Always Bannock had believed that every woman has her price. And he laughed when they told him to keep away from the beautiful Samoan tribal virgin....

TRANSLATED FROM the liquid sibilance of the Samoan tongue, her name meant Crimson Lily.

She was the half-caste daughter of a white father and an island mother; and she was like an ivory flame. The very sight of her was enough to set a man's veins afire; yet there was something queer about her, too—a faint, sinister aura that somehow chilled you and warned you to keep your distance. Hers was the fascination of a beautiful orchid whose heart exudes a mysterious and fatal poison.

Kendrick Bannock first saw her the night his palatial yacht dropped anchor in the coral harbor of Pangatonga. He saw her, and immediately he desired her and whatever Kendrick Bannock desired of life, he managed to get—come hell or high water. He was a ruthless man.

Vreeland, the Dutch trader with the Oxonian accent, who ran the general store at Pangatonga, gave Kendrick Bannock fair warning that first night. "You steer clear of that Crimson Lily girl, mister," he said tersely.

"Why should I?" Bannock demanded. He had consumed too many pegs of whiskey-soda since anchoring in the harbor; and he was more than a little truculent. Much wealth had given Kendrick Bannock an imperious arrogance. He thought of himself as only a little less powerful than God.

Vreeland, the trader, shrugged. "The girl's *taupoo*—which means that she's the tribal virgin. It's a part of the Samoan religion; like the ancient vestals of Rome, y'know. To touch her is *tabu*—strict-

74

ly and absolutely forbidden. If you were to make a play for her, the witch-doctors would put a curse on you that'd haunt you to your grave."

"Nonsense!" Kendrick Bannock scoffed. "I suppose you'll be telling me next that the girl herself might cast a spell over me that would shrivel my soul or something."

"She might, at that!" Vreeland said quietly.

"You're a fool!" Bannock grunted. "There's no such thing as witchcraft or magic, and you know it."

"I've lived in the South Seas for twenty-odd years," Vreeland said. "And I've learned to keep an open mind. I've seen queer things happen."

Bannock merely laughed contemptuously. Then he went out to watch the dancing.

IT was the night of the full moon, which is also the night of the *taupoo* dance—the dance of the virgin. In the very center of the Samoan village compound there was a cleared space, the dancing-ground.

All about the cleared place, squatting natives hunkered. Their faces gleamed like brown, savage wraiths in the flickering light of the coconut torches. There was something weird and barbaric about the scene; something that made Kendrick Bannock shudder, in spite of himself. Yet he was perspiring through his thin suit of China silk.

Perhaps it was the music, he told himself irritably. Shrill and wailing, the bamboo pipes squealed their harsh dissonances. And above the wailing, the drums thudded monotonously. *Thud*-thump-tunk-thunk-a-tump. *Thud*-thump-tunk-thunk-a-thump. Over and over again, until a man's nerves were worn raw.

"Damned swinish savages!" Kendrick Bannock growled.

Suddenly, from one of the frond-thatched huts, a witch-doctor leaped into the clearing. On his head he wore a huge, gargoyle mask, studded with feathers and fantastically horrible with crimson and ocher paints. The thing was fashioned to resemble a huge, grinning skull; and from the eye-sockets, the man's yellow orbs gleamed eerily.

For a moment he stood there, posturing. Then from his throat issued a crepitant, marrow-congealing moan—a gibbering sound that struck terror into a man's immortal soul. It was the signal for Crimson Lily, the Virgin, to come forth and dance.

Out of the shadows she glided; and at sight of her, Kendrick Bannock's pulses began to leap and race, even as they had leaped and raced when first he had seen her earlier that evening. God, she was beautiful, he told himself.

She wore nothing but a native *pareu*—a typical island tunic of flower-printed red silk, thin and gossamer and revealing. It was draped about her in such fashion that one of her firm young breasts was uncovered; and Kendrick Bannock's eyes rested hungrily upon the soft allure of the girl's body.

His glance raced over the rest of her slim young form. Her brown legs were tapered and exquisite; her thighs warm and gleaming and lithe. Her hips swayed cat-like as she danced; and her waist was narrow, supple. The poetry of her movements got into Kendrick Bannock's blood like a raging fever. He began to pant....

HE and Vreeland, the Dutch trader, were the only *papalengi*— the only white men—watching that *taupoo* dance. And at first the girl, Crimson Lily, paid them no heed.

But gradually, something of Bannock's snake-like fixed stare must have penetrated her consciousness; for she turned her dark-glowing eyes upon him. Their gazes met—and locked.

At the impact of her eyes, Kendrick Bannock felt a cold and worm-like shiver crawling along his spine; he didn't know why. It was as if his flesh had suddenly been festooned with suppurating maggots. Sweat began to stand out in viscid globules on his forehead. Almost desperately he forced himself to return Crimson Lily's ophidian stare.

For a long moment he no longer saw her body; no longer could discern the lilting curves of her thighs, the enticing cones of her breasts. He saw only her eyes—and they seemed filled with a hell-erupted light. For the first time in his life, Kendrick Bannock thought he knew the meaning of fear.

He fought the sensation back. Damn such tommyrot! No half-breed wench could stare him down! He glared into her eyes; forced a malicious, sardonic grin to his lips. At the same moment, a feeling of rage rose up in his throat. From the very first, he had wanted her. That had been infatuation. But now—

Now he wanted to crush her in his arms, maul her, hurt her, dominate her physically, for another reason. He wanted to hurt her irreparably, out of sheer savage hate. Just as a man might pluck a flower by the roots and smash it to a bruised pulp....

Almost it seemed as if she had read his thoughts; for a new light leaped into her strange eyes. A light of combat, of mocking challenge. She seemed to be pitting her will against his own; seemed to be taunting him, telling him that his strength was nothing but pitiable weakness compared to her own half-savage superiority. Her very smile was a threat.

The full malignance of her gaze daggered into Kendrick Bannock's soul; it was almost like a physical blow. Despite himself, he lowered his eyes. The girl had stared him down!

And then he thought he heard her laughing at him; though he knew full well that no sound had issued from her sardonic, kiss-crimson lips.

HE felt the touch of Vreeland, the trader, on his shoulder; and he turned irritably. "What do you want?" he snarled.

"You're bleeding!" Vreeland said quietly. "Your mouth is bloody."

Then, and only then, did Kendrick Bannock realize that his

teeth had bitten through his own lower lip until the blood had come.

He forced himself to laugh. He mopped his forehead, dabbed at his mouth with the handkerchief. "Need a drink!" he muttered darkly. "This damned dancing gets on my nerves. Come on—let's get out of here!"

Vreeland nodded absently. "As you wish," he said.

Together they went back to the trading post. Bannock downed four stiff tots of gin in succession. But the fiery stuff didn't help very much. He felt queerly drained, as if the *taupoo*-girl, Crimson Lily, had established a psychic liaison with his soul—and through that liaison had sapped his strength.

He banged down his gin-glass. "That girl, Crimson Lily—" he said.

"Yes?" Vreeland's voice was quiet. "Still thinking about her, even after what happened out there?"

"What do you mean? What are you talking about?" Kendrick Bannock growled.

"Nothing happened outside, that I was aware of!"

Vreeland was not a man to be browbeaten, even by a millionaire like Kendrick Bannock. "I refer," the trader said gently, "to the way she stared you down." Then he smiled. "It's quite evident that Crimson Lily hates your guts, Bannock."

Bannock flushed brick-red. "To hell with her hate!" he rasped. "I want her, and I mean to have her! How much will it cost?"

"Cost?" Vreeland said slowly. "I don't understand."

"Like hell you don't understand!" Bannock sneered. "All these native wenches have a price. I'll pay her parents whatever they demand, just for the privilege of taking Crimson Lily aboard my tub for one single night." The millionaire's lips peeled back from his strong white teeth. "I'll wager it'll be a night she'll long remember!"

Vreeland shook his head gravely. "You're off on the wrong foot, mister. In the first place, Crimson Lily's parents are both dead. She's in the care of the native tribal witch-doctors. Moreover, I've told you she's *taupoo*—the tribe's official virgin. She's not to be had; not for any amount of money."

"That's a lie!" Bannock rasped. "There isn't a woman in the whole damned world, who can't be bought for gold!"

VREELAND smiled. "You're quite wrong—and rather offensive into the bargain, Bannock. Let me repeat my warning, while overlooking your crassness. That girl, Crimson Lily, is *taupoo*. If you make any attempt to harm her, they'll put a spell on you that'll send your soul shrieking into hell. And I mean just that. I'm not spoofing you one tot."

Kendrick Bannock swayed to his feet. He was more than a bit drunk; and his mood was ugly. "I refuse to be frightened by ghost-stories!" he snarled. "Good night, Vreeland. And I hope you have nightmares about witch-doctors and curses and all the rest of your superstitious drivel."

Vreeland grinned. "Good night, mister."

Bannock walked unsteadily out into the moon-silvered night. The world seemed electroplated by the glow of moon and stars; the Southern Cross blazed hotly, high overhead.

Over toward the native village, the dancing had ceased. The coconut flares had died; the Samoans had vanished. The silence was almost strident in its dead stillness; and there seemed to be an evil lurking in the air. Kendrick Bannock shivered, cursed.

He strode toward the slip that jutted into the coral harbor. His launch was waiting there. But just as he reached the water's edge, he heard a sound.

It was a faint splashing, as of a sleek body cutting smoothly through the mirror-calm, tiny harbor. In the moonlight, Bannock suddenly saw a brown-ivory shape swimming toward him.

He crouched in the shadows. Abrupt perspiration trickled from his armpits. It was the girl, Crimson Lily… and she was emerging from the water like a dripping, haunting naiad.

Her coal-dark hair streamed wetly around her shoulders, framing the savage beauty of her face, the sun tanned breasts that rose and fell with each hurried breath. She had twisted her *pareu* about her middle, like a loin-cloth; and save for this flimsy garment she was completely nude.

"God!" Kendrick Bannock whispered hoarsely. And his veins leaped with angry desire for her. In the moonlight, he could see plainly outlined the rounded loveliness of her breasts, the redness of her full lips. The soaked *pareu* clung to her hips, sleekly molded her slim thighs. There was enticement in every nuance of her body; and Bannock seethed with abrupt, atavistic passion-urges.

Yet over those churning urges of the flesh, there came a sudden incomprehensible dread festering in his hard soul. A dread completely inexplicable; a hell-inspired fear that grew like a cancer as Crimson Lily came closer to his place of concealment.

It was strange, terrifying, the struggle that now took place in Kendrick Bannock's being. A part of him seemed fiendishly eager to leap forward, grab the half-caste girl and bend her to his will. But another part of him recoiled from the thought, as a man might recoil from embracing a hideous and deadly cobra.

HE tried to tell himself that it was all crazy, this damned fool dread that rose within him like a slime-viscous tide to drown his courage. He tried to tell himself that Vreeland, the trader, must have hypnotized him with his droning talk of witch-doctors and hell-curses. It was all nonsense!

Yes, but what about the way the girl, Crimson Lily, had stared him down? What about the way her eyes had glared into his when she performed her *taupoo*-dance? He tried to make himself believe that it had been because of the smoke from the guttering coconut torches.

Yes; that was it! The smoke had got into his eyes; that's why Crimson Lily had been able to stare him down! Otherwise no half-breed island slut could outface him, the great and mighty Kendrick Bannock! Nor, he decided, could any brown-skinned wench deny him pleasure, if he felt like demanding it.

Blustering, Bannock stepped out from the shadows; came face to face with Crimson Lily. "See here!" he rasped.

She seemed neither startled nor frightened. She merely stopped dead in her tracks; and her peculiar eyes lit up with a queer glow.

"Ah. The strange *papalengi* from the yacht!" she said softly.

"You don't seem surprised to see me," Bannock growled.

Somehow, he had hoped to frighten her by his sudden appearance had hoped to startle some of the arrogance out of her. But the trick hadn't worked. Instead, it was he, Kendrick Bannock, who began to experience a sudden, growing disquiet.

The girl shrugged indifferently. "No. I am not surprised. I had a feeling that you would be here, somewhere, waiting for me." With studied insolence she unwrapped her wet *pareu* from about her hips; and for a single instant stood there as if to expose herself to him utterly unclad, as beautiful as a pagan goddess. Then she adjusted the wet, clinging silk snugly so that it covered her completely from armpits to knees.

Kendrick Bannock licked his thick lips greasily. "I like you better without that damned rag!" he said. And he reached forward, grasped at the *pareu,* tried to yank it away from her.

The silk tore, so that

"I could cast a spell on you for that," she told him.

her nubile breasts were half revealed in the moonlight. And then Crimson Lily laughed!

The sound of that unexpected, ululant laughter knifed into Bannock's brain like a white-hot scalpel of pain. There was amusement in it, and mocking contempt. Then, abruptly, the girl's eyes narrowed.

She snatched at the tatters of the *pareu,* held it before her bosom. "I would not advise you to do that again, sir," she spoke softly, venomously.

Kendrick Bannock took a step toward her. "And why not?" he leered. "I happen to like the looks of you. I want you. I intend to have you. There'll be a nice bit of money in it for you, of course," he added casually.

Crimson Lily drew a sharp breath. "You—you dare offer me money…?"

Bannock smiled. "I don't ask for free kisses. I pay as I go," he said. This was his code; his law. This was the precept by which he lived. And what in hell was wrong with it?

THE half-caste girl looked at him as if he had been some new species of invertebrate. "Do you realize that I could cast a spell upon you for that insult?" she whispered savagely.

Kendrick Bannock started to laugh in her face; and then, abruptly, the sound died in his throat. He took a staggering, backward step. Crimson Lily's eyes were blazing into his own; searing his brain. He felt his strength flowing from him. He felt engulfed in some weird, hellish power that was rending and tearing at his immortal soul, even as he had torn the half-caste girl's *pareu* a moment ago.

He could feel the cold sweat pouring from his temples, running down his cheeks. "God—don't look at me that way!" he gasped thickly.

"So you fear me, after all!" Crimson Lily whispered mockingly. Then, deliberately, she turned her back upon him and slithered away through the moonlight.

Bannock sank weakly down upon the jutting dock; and his belly seemed strangely nauseated.

A LONG time he must have remained there; a long, numbed time, because the moon was far down on the sea's flat horizon when at last he found the volition to stand upon his feet once more.

God in heaven—what was happening to him? What foul hypnosis had the girl cast upon him, to destroy his will and his manhood so utterly? A quick red rage flashed upward into his brain. That girl, Crimson Lily, damn her soul to hell's black fires! She had outfaced him again; had met his challenge, bested him in a battle of psychic forces!

And now a vindictive hatred seethed in Kendrick Bannock's heart. He would have Crimson Lily! By God, he would have her, take her, sate himself with her femininity! He would destroy her soul! It was the only way in which he could regain the shards of his self-respect.

Grimly he turned and started toward the native village, through the lateness of the deserted night.

But with his every forward step, a voice seemed to be whispering in his ear; a voice whispering of danger, of peril, of dread. He felt the congealing ooze of nameless terror creeping through his veins, frigidly. His legs seemed weak under him.

Yet doggedly he kept on. His hate was greater than his fear; and his passion surpassed both.

He was panting, now; panting with anticipation of holding Crimson Lily in his arms, crushing her against him, mauling her daintiness with his thick, esurient fingers. He would kiss her lips, her shoulders, her throat. He would triumph over her, the damned half-breed slut! And when he had finished with her, he would smash his fist into her face.

He reached the palm-thatched hut where Crimson Lily lived.

Cautiously, soundlessly, he approached the tiny native structure. Ruthlessly he throttled back the strange terror that welled up from his guts. He neared the front-thatched hut—

"Well, by God!" he whispered in sheer amazement. And a savage, berserk jealousy crowded through the interstices of his flinty soul.

WITHIN Crimson Lily's hut, a tiny light gleamed. There was a chink in the wall; and through it, Bannock could peer into the dwelling's single room. He stared.

He stared, and saw Crimson Lily in the arms of a tall, broad-shouldered native. The girl's *pareu* draped loosely, ineffectually about her, hardly concealing her loveliness; and the man was caressing her... with the gentle, possessive touch of a lover.

"Let us go away together to some small island!" the native was whispering to Crimson Lily. "Let us hide forever from our tribes-men. Together we will face the wrath which our gods have seen fit to plague us. Together we will live, and die, with our love."

The *taupoo*-girl pushed the man away. "Not yet, my lover. Not yet!" she answered dreamily. "I have a feeling that it is not to be. A more evil ending awaits us…. And who are we to question the decisions of the gods of our ancestors?"

Reluctantly, the tall, broad-shouldered native released Crimson Lily from his embrace. For a last time he kissed her gently. Then he turned his face and strode out of the hut.

And in the shadowy darkness outside, Kendrick Bannock suddenly grinned an evil, malign grin. So that was it! Crimson Lily, the *taupoo*-girl; the tribe's professional virgin… entertaining a man in her hut! What a monstrous jest it was! She, the virgin, had refused Kendrick Bannock's proferred love; had spurned his money. Yet she gave herself to this Kanaka native!

Bannock's hand stole to his pocket; came forth with a gold-encrusted folding knife. He flicked out the blade; crouched. The tall native had to pass him in the darkness. He waited. Waited until the man was within two feet of him. And then Kendrick Bannock leaped.

The knife flashed metallically; and there was no more metallic glitter, because the blade was buried in the native's back. And when it was withdrawn, the steel was red with blood. Again and again Bannock struck.

Panting, he looked down at last upon the body of the man he had murdered. Not that he gave a damn about the actual slaying. What was one more Samoan, more or less?

He straightened up; turned. He made for the doorway of Crimson Lily's hut. He stepped inside.

The girl cried out as he entered. She leaped to her feet, clutched her *pareu* about her in a vain effort to cover her alluring nakedness. "You!" she whispered.

KENDRICK BANNOCK laughed throatily. "Yes. Me. I've just killed your boy-friend."

The *taupoo*-girl's ivory features went pale. "You—you have slain the man who was in here with me?"

"Right. And now, how would you like me to go to your witch-doctor and tell him what I saw? How would you like to have me spill the beans about that chap holding you in his arms, kissing you, fondling you, doing God knows what?"

The girl's eyes narrowed. "If you told that, they would put me to death—by torture!" she answered slowly.

Kendrick Bannock's lips parted in a sardonic smile. "Not a very pleasant prospect, is it?" he taunted her.

Crimson Lily was silent.

Bannock pressed his advantage; because it was not in his nature to do otherwise. Leaping desires were beginning to course through him; surging yearnings. He wanted Crimson Lily, wanted her with a white-hot longing. "I wouldn't give you away if you were to be nice to me," he said.

"Nice to you?"

"Yes. Come with me now, out to my yacht in the lagoon. I won't make you stay beyond sunrise. Nobody need ever know that you visited me."

She looked at him queerly, speculatively. "You are a man who usually gets what he wants, aren't you?"

"Not usually. Invariably!" Bannock corrected her arrogantly. "I always get what I go after. And this time, I'm after you."

Once again she looked at him. Something slithered in her eyes—something of hate, of loathing, of surrender… and of impending triumph. It was a queer, enigmatic look; and it sent a shudder through Bannock's marrow.

The girl spoke. "If you force me to your will, a curse will be upon you. It will bring death to you. Horrible death!" she intoned weirdly.

Bannock laughed. "More of your superstitious bosh!" he scoffed. "I refuse to be frightened by spells and charms and incantantions!"

Crimson Lily wrapped her silken *pareu* tightly about her lithe body. "Very well," she said quietly. "The risk is yours."

TOGETHER they went out into the dark night. The moon was gone; and there remained only the blazing stars. The girl darted one swift glance toward the corpse of the native man whom Kendrick Bannock had slain. Just one glance. Then she turned away silently. And she went with Bannock to his launch.

Aboard the yacht, he led her to the deserted afterdeck. He switched on a single shaded light, under the canopy. He clasped Crimson Lily about the waist; drew her toward him.

She came without protest; and now the hot fires of desire in Bannock's veins mounted to leaping, savage fury. He rained kisses upon her moist, humid lips. He tore at her *pareu,* so that he could crush and flatten her against him. With his greedy eyes he drank in the glories of her half-clad body.

Then she backed away from him. "I shall dance for you!" she smiled.

"No. I don't like your *taupoo*-dance. The dance of the virgin! Rot!" His tone was stinging sarcasm, for he was remembering the man who had been with her in her hut; the man he had murdered.

Crimson Lily smiled again. "Not the *taupoo*-dance. The *siva-siva.* The love-dance. The mating dance."

"Well, that sounds better!" Bannock grinned. "Go ahead."

And she danced. Exotically, temptingly, provocatively. Her hips swayed, and her firm breasts. Every posture was a daring invitation, a seductive promise. Her hands undulated along her gleaming, writhing hips. Her long fingers moved caressingly over the flesh of her bared breasts, and the gesture maddened him. Sinuously, passionately, she danced as if to the unheard rhythms of some barbaric music.

And with every movement of her body, the flaming flowing lava of molten desire seethed higher through Kendrick Bannock's soul. Gone now was all his former fear of her; vanished was his trepidation and his dread. Yet had he only known it, there was a fouler evil closing in on him than he could ever dream.

At last he could wait no longer. He sprang at Crimson Lily; lifted her from her feet. Savagely, almost insanely, he flung her upon the upholstery-cushioned bench at the afterrail....

LONG moments later she looked at him mistily, weirdly. "Now we must seal our passion in blood!" she whispered.

"In blood?"

"Yes. I will show you." She slipped her hand into his pocket; withdrew his knife—the knife with which he had slain her native lover. She opened the stained blade.

Bannock drew back. "What's this?" he rasped. "If you think you can play any tricks—"

"It is no trick. You are my man; my blood-mate. Our union has been made; but now it must be sealed in blood. See... there is no hurt." And she sliced a tiny incision upon the flesh of her rounded forearm.

Warm blood flowed slowly. It was a small cut, almost imperceptible. Kendrick Bannock's lips peeled back in a soft laugh of superiority. "Native stuff, eh? Witchcraft marriage? Well, I'm not afraid! Go ahead—seal our mating in blood if you want to!"

She took his wrist, nicked his flesh. To the small, bleeding wound she had made in his arm, she now applied her own flesh—exactly where she had cut herself. She rubbed the incisions together, one upon the other, so that their blood was intermingled.

Then she smiled slowly. "Now we are one!" she whispered. "Now your blood is my blood, and my blood is yours. I have taken your strength and your weaknesses; and now you share my own weaknesses, my own power. It is written."

Kendrick Bannock laughed again. Strange, he thought, how he had once feared this girl. How she had inspired a congealing slime of horror within him. But now—hell! She was just another dame. And he was weary of her.

"You'd better get back to shore," he said gruffly. "I'm tired. I want to go to bed."

"Yes. You are right. I must leave you now. It is time for me to go to my gods...."

Bannock didn't quite understand the full import of her words just then. He thought she meant she must return to the witch-doctors in the village, on the island. Watching her as she slipped over the rail and into the water, he had no inkling of her real meaning.

He did not even watch her as she swam to the shore of the lagoon; did not see her as she walked slowly toward her hut.

IT was early the next morning when he learned the truth. At sunrise, to be exact. Just as the sun's orange disc climbed over the far horizon, Kendrick Bannock had a visitor to his yacht

It was Vreeland, the trader.

Vreeland looked disturbed. He insisted that Bannock be wakened; said he wanted to talk with the millionaire.

A steward finally ac-

Suddenly he drove the knife into the native's back.

quiesced; knocked on Bannock's door. Bannock poked his head out into the new sunshine. "What's up?" he growled surlily.

Vreeland spoke softly. "I thought you might like to hear the news. A native was murdered last night—nobody knows who did it. But it develops that the chap was Crimson Lily's secret lover. And Crimson Lily herself has committed suicide."

Kendrick Bannock stiffened. "Suicide?"

"Yes. They found her body in her hut, a little while ago. Poor child; perhaps it was better that she and her lover died together. I made a hasty medical examination of the two corpses, a few minutes ago. I discovered that they were both *lepers!*"

"Lepers?" Bannock choked.

"Yes. The disease was just beginning to show its silver scales on their bodies. That's why I say it's probably best that they died."

"Lepers—leprosy... *oh, my God!*" Kendrick Bannock whispered. Abruptly he remembered something that had happened last night. Crimson Lily, slicing her own flesh and the flesh of Bannock. Intermingling their bloods. Telling him that her power would be his power; *and her weakness, his weakness!*

The curse of the *taupoo!* The curse that would send him to his grave, haunt him to his death, horribly, as she had predicted! She had known it, all the time; had warned him. And he had been too blind to heed her! He remembered hearing that native chap talking to her in her hut; urging her to run away with him. There had been something about the wrath of the gods. Then both of them must have known of their condition!

The curse of the *taupoo!* Leprosy! In Kendrick Bannock's bloodstream! *Silver scales....*

"God in Heaven!" Kendrick Bannock sobbed. And he stared down at the knife-wound in his arm.

CLINT MORGAN

BLIND FLIGHT

*In the plane's cabin rode hate, cupidity, lust—all
the seven deadly sins! Male and female, they
were an evil freight. And at the controls was...?*

INSIDE **the small** *station of the Interstate Airways....
Three men disconsolately sitting about a table; three men clad in
the blue whipcord and leather puttees of pilots.... Silver wings gleaming on each chest....*

Outside, thick, impenetrable fog pressed down like a suffocating blanket of fleece.

"Zero-zero," muttered the first, the oldest of the flyers. "It's a laugh. The mail must go through, but a little soupy fog keeps it on the ground!"

"Three days," said the second. "Not a plane in or out in three days."

The third, the youngest of the trio, gazed at the wet window. "It's got to let up," he groaned. "Mac's dying in the hospital by inches and his girl can't get to him! He's hanging on, waiting, waiting, and this damn' fog—"

"Dickie," broke in the first, "quit worrying about the dame. It won't help. Mac is done for; he's in pain. He'd be better off dead; poor devil. She can never make it through this fog!"

The sound of the radio broke in on the conversation.

"Calling Interstate Airways, Chicago, Interstate Airways, Chicago."

One of the men grabbed for the instruments. Another said, "For the love of God, what crazy fool is up in weather like this? The devil himself couldn't make it with fog that—"

WITHIN *a city apartment.... John Knox sipping his drink*

thoughtfully, swarthy face reddening a little as he listened to the woman's words.

She paced the floor dramatically, a cigarette in one hand, a glass in the other. The thin negligee clung to her hips, liquid and provocative, like wet tissue paper. One white leg at a time emerged from the folds of the garment as she walked. Her breasts almost half revealed by the lowcut throat, surged and quivered alluringly. John Knox licked his lips.

"Surely you can see the wisdom in my words, John! I'm no ordinary kept woman. If you had told me at the start that you had a wife, it might have been different. But I can't let myself break up a family since I've found out the truth."

Knox set his glass carefully on the table, dabbed at his lips with

a silk handkerchief, and smiled. His smile was hardly pleasant, his lips too grim and thinned, his eyes too narrowed, too burning.

"So this is goodbye?" he asked.

She shrugged, turned slotted green eyes his way. "What else can it be? I can't and won't break up your wife's home!"

Now he was on his feet walking slowly toward her. "Then make it a real goodbye, Helen," he said softly and before she could move, swept her into his arms. Her breasts pressed his, her whole figure flattened against his own. Back, back over the table he pressed her, his lips hungrily on hers. Her eyes closed, her lips parted, she sighed, wound her own arms about his neck. Suddenly his mouth broke away.

"Goodbye, goodbye," he muttered, "but not goodbye like you think! *This* is goodbye, Helen, and *this!*"

His fist crashed into her face. Blood spurted from her battered nose, from a cut above her eyebrow. She screamed once—only once—then relaxed, unconscious. Her last conscious knowledge had been that she was staring straight upward into the eyes of a demented man.

His voice arose to a shriek, a cry of anguish. "Goodbye, goodbye, is it? Am I mad? Am I crazy, a fool that I can't see through you? I knew a week ago that you were through with me, you harlot! You've bled me for everything I had, drained me dry. You're not worrying about my wife; it's my money that makes you say goodbye!"

GREAT angry splotches of red were seeping from beneath his closing fingers. The white throat in his grip changed color, began to blacken beneath the pressure. Her mouth came open, she gasped for air, clawed feebly at the iron bands of his fingers. Still muttering, still sobbing he increased the pressure. Presently her long, lithe body twitched once, twice and lay still. With a sob he wrenched at the negligee. No longer those pointed breasts rose and fell, no longer that flat waist quivered with life.

"I love you, I love you," he sobbed and started back. The body of the dead woman swayed, rolled from the table to collapse grotesquely on the floor.

"Helen, Helen!" he gasped. Suddenly he leaned over her, picked her up in his arms and staggered toward the bedroom. Like a child with a doll, a mother with a baby he arranged the still form on the bed. Statuesque, superb in its lines, it lay twisted in the semblance of a smile. For a long while John Knox stared down at the body of the woman he had loved and killed.

"Goodbye, goodbye," he said thickly and leaned to kiss a dark hollow in her throat. On lagging, uncertain feet he hurried from the bedroom, stopped in the hallway for his hat and coat, then headed for the Scotch bottle that sat on the library table. The whiskey felt warm, invigorating. He eyed the bottle crazily, slipped it into his overcoat pocket. At the door he stopped to turn out the lights.

"Goodbye, goodbye," he muttered and stepped out into the fog that hung over the quiet streets like a woollen coverlet. His car was at the curb.

IN *another apartment: a man and a woman....*

Joe Bloom was short, fat and hairy. In his violently purple shirt, he looked like a benevolent, modernized Guatama Buddha. The woman by the dressing table, clad in the thinnest of sheer silk nightgowns watched him with veiled amusement in her eyes. He reached for his vest, pulled it over the loud suspenders that hung on his fat shoulders.

"You're not sorry, are you, daddykins?"

Joe grinned coyly, winked an eye at the shapely one. "Sorry? I should be sorry when by waiting I have time to spend with you? Late! Of course, your Joey is late, but I can catch a plane."

"And you're not sorry you stayed over?" One long slender leg slid from the negligee as she moved quickly and walked toward him. The sheerness of the garment accented the flaring curve of her hips, the tapering beauty of her chiseled thighs. Her breasts, plainly revealed through the chiffon, swayed and quivered. He reached for her with a hairy hand.

"Momma," he grinned, "how can you say it? It's been the happiest time of Joe Bloom's life! I can't get over it yet, a swell baby like you loving an old ape like Joe!"

He enfolded her possessively with pudgy arms. As his fat lips touched her throat, her own mouth made a grimace of distaste; she tensed, then caught herself in time and simulated pleasure. Joe Bloom breathed hard as her soft loveliness, svelte and scented pressed against his own grotesqueness. His pudgy hands reached, found soft flesh, warm and poignant.

"Don't leave me, daddykins," she murmured huskily.

PRESENTLY he thrust her gently aside. "I got to catch my plane, honey. I've got to be in Chi by tomorrow morning if I'm going to sell Rader those stones. But I'll be back, don't worry, I'll be back."

The stiff collar next, then the brilliant tie with its glaring diamond below the knot. She lit a cigarette and regarded him

The plane swooped, she grabbed for a strut, then missed and hurtled downward....

gravely as he buttoned his vest. Chattering like a great ape he threw a few toilet articles into a bag, searched through the bureau drawer and came out with a black case. He opened the case, leaned over it, touched its contents lovingly with a pudgy finger. She came swiftly to him, leaned over his shoulder and peered down at the bureau top. Her breasts rose and fell; she breathed audibly.

"God," she said, "they're lovely, daddykins."

Joe Bloom grinned. "Not bad, baby. Twenty-four rocks for

Rader. I'm hoping he'll buy them. Daddy's commission will mean things for you. Now be sweet and call a cab."

He put the black case of cut diamonds into his inside coat pocket, adjusted a jaunty derby on his bald head and surveyed himself with satisfaction in the mirror.

Presently, waiting for a cab, he sat in the deep stuffed chair, the scantily clad woman in his lap. Their talk was ridiculous. She kissed him, pressed against him, ran her hands over his pudginess. Joe Bloom breathed, sighed happily. She touched the black case in his pocket and her eyes grew avid, greedy. She pressed her too red lips hard against his, pressed her white body against his pudgy flesh, thrilled as she felt the hard bulge of the black case burning into the softness of her breast.

The bell rang. "It's the cab, baby," said Joe and arose, seized his gladstone. There was a short farewell at the door, then he was gone. The pudgy figure of a little philanderer caught in the net of a siren and Circe with eighty thousand dollars' worth of cut diamonds in his inner pocket.

The woman hurried to the front window of the bedroom. Quickly she raised and lowered the shade three times, waited a minute and repeated the maneuver.

Across the street Soapy Turco, slumped beneath the wheel of the lightless sedan, saw the shade go up and down. His eyes narrowed, his lips grew thinner. Softly he started his own car without switching on the lights. The fog was so thick he could hardly make out the pudgy figure as it came from the apartment house door, entered the waiting cab.

Soapy turned the black roadster around, kept close to the red flickering tail light of the Yellow. It wasn't hard to follow because the fog was so heavy that the cab driver was afraid to speed up. As Soapy drove, he felt once beneath his left arm to see if the long, keen knife still nestled there. It did.

ACROSS the city—*in a woman's boudoir….*

The phone rang. *"Whrrrrrrrrrrrrr!"*

The man released the woman and said, "Damn it! Let it ring!"

She was tall and svelte, her head crowned with a glorious sheen of platinum hair. She laughed as she shrugged back into a shoulder strap, recovering completely a too generous breast. As she arose, her skirt dropped into place from its former position at her knee. She shrugged down into its caressing folds, smoothed it over full hips, dodged the playfully slapping hand of her lover, and went to the phone.

"Yes? All right I'll take it. This is Mrs. Ashton." She winked at the man who had struggled up to pour two drinks. "It's George," she whispered, hand over the mouthpiece, "old Santa Claus himself calling from Chicago!" The man grinned, gulped a drink, handed to her which she waved aside, cooing into the telephone, "Hello, hello, honey! Just fine, how are you?"

For the next five minutes she conducted her end of the conversation with many a term of endearment, many a coy promise. All the time she winked at the man on the divan, who helped himself to more liquor and grimaced at his mistress.

"All right, lover, in the morning then," she concluded and made a kissing noise into the phone. The receiver clicked into place. Slowly she took her drink, sipped it, eyeing her lover askance.

"Well," he muttered, "what does the old goat want now?"

She hesitated. "He wants me to fly out there and spend the week-end with him. Listen, honey—"

The man was on his feet; his eyes angry. "What the hell do you think I am? If you think I'm going to sit on the nest and keep the eggs warm while you play around with your old man, you're crazy!" His voice was scornful. She hastened toward him, placed a white full arm about his neck. He tried to thrust her aside but she pleaded with him.

"Don't be angry, darling. You know we're almost out of money. I can talk him out of plenty during the week-end. I'll buy you that roadster, darling, that one you've been wanting so badly."

His eyes grew shrewd. His arms enfolded her, drew her to him. Almost thoughtlessly he kissed her, caressed her, slipped the shoulder strap from her white shoulder again. She breathed deeply, closed her own eyes and held him close.

Presently he said, "If you must, you must. But don't forget to leave me some money."

AN HOUR later he sat watching her dress. After all, he reflected, she wasn't so damned old. Her figure was still good, thanks to massage and reducing diets. And what the hell? The old dame had jack!

She opened a box on her bureau. "I think this will keep you till I get back, Jackie," she murmured and laid three hundred-dollar bills in his palm. She looked at him quizzically, saw the petulant look in his eyes and quickly laid another beside the first three. He smiled.

"You're sweet," he said and swept her into his arms. She moaned a little, parted her rouged lips, and sought his mouth. Her caress was avid, her arms all enveloping.

A half hour later he got out of a cab after telling the mink-coated woman farewell for the last time. The fog was so thick that he could scarcely see the whiteness of her waving hand as the cab disappeared, but the wavering glow of a street light danced and gleamed on the facets of her many rings.

He grimaced, stepped into a cigar store and made for the telephone booth. Presently he got his party, said, "What have I been doing? I've been working, kid, working like hell. Slip on a dress and meet me at the corner of Eleventh and Thames. We'll have a little party."

Across town Mrs. Inez Ashton was replacing her makeup as well as she could in the dim light and wondering just how she would persuade her husband to give her an additional ten thousand dollars.

BACK in the Interstate Airways office, five people listened to Joe Bloom pound on the counter. "Do you mean to tell me that on account of a little fog we can't get a plane out of here? Do you mean to tell me—?"

Patiently the man in the blue whipcords explained. "This is zero-zero weather, sir. We could get you off, but the fog is lying so close all over the country east of the Mississippi that you'd never land. I'm sorry; that's final. We've turned down at least a hundred reservations, but that's the best we can do. Safety comes first."

Soapy Turco, hardened killer, slumped back whimpering as the pilot lifted his goggles.

Seated dejectedly in a corner, gnawing at his nails John Knox's red-rimmed eyes were burning into the floor. In his mind he was seeing a vision of the woman he had murdered, stretched out white, nude, and still in the room he had paid for. His fingers twitched as if he still felt the soft flesh yielding and bruising beneath them. With trembling hands he lighted another cigarette, dragged hard on it, and tossed it impatiently aside. From a distance he heard the man's words, "—impossible sir—sorry—not safe—"

Knox leaped to his feet and paced the floor. Flight! Anywhere, any place away from here.

Mrs. Inez Ashton leaned indolently against the counter and applied lipstick to her full lips. She was thinking of Jackie, cursing at the fog that would make her journey one day longer. Get to

Chicago and get that week-end over with!

Soapy Turco, cleaning his nails industriously with his head bent low, eyed her round sleek figure with approval, and cast a wary eye from time to time on the pudgy figure of Joe Bloom.

Behind the stove a man in a yellow overcoat half crouched in a seat, a leather bound parcel perhaps eighteen inches square between his legs. He peered about through thick-rimmed glasses at the assemblage, gnawed at his black moustache and bit at his nails.

Opposite him, Marion Shipley, petite and blonde, praying for her lover who lay in a hospital in Chicago, railing at the fog that kept her from his side.

Joe Bloom snorted in disgust, wheeled about, and walked out of the office. Soapy quickly put the nailfile away, waited a moment and followed. Outside, the fog was so dense that vision was blocked at a distance of six feet. He could just make out the pudgy figure of the diamond salesman. His hand sought and found the hilt of his knife. His lips tightened. Now was the time!

Thud!

Joe Bloom snorted, said, "Excuse it, please, a fellow can't see!"

A new voice broke in, low and colorless, "Yeah, tough weather. Listen, I couldn't help overhearing the conversation in the office. I've got my own ship, partner, and I need money. Don't say anything to the flyers in the office but, if you guys can raise a grand among you, I'll fly the whole bunch to Chicago, fog or no fog."

Soapy drew back into the deeper shadows, listened to the diamond salesman's anxious voice. He cursed as the pudgy one detached himself from his chance companion and hurried back into the office, where he began talking *sotto voce* to those assembled. Damn it! Well, there was nothing else to do. If the salesman flew west, Soapy would fly west too. Somewhere before they landed or afterwards he'd get a chance to relieve the man of a fortune in diamonds.

TEN minutes later the group stood on the tarmac outside a vague hangar while the mysterious pilot wheeled a heavy ship onto the cement. They sensed rather than saw each other, for the fog was down like a fleecy cloud.

"All right," said the man in the coveralls, tugging his helmet well down over his eyes.

One by one they entered. Joe Bloom sat well forward; Soapy Turco smiled and sank into a seat behind him. Inez Ashton sailed majestically aboard, took a seat amidships, and crossed her legs with a great revealing flourish. The man in the yellow coat paused briefly beside her, looked down at the shimmering chiffon, the scant ribbon of bare flesh topping it. She smiled deliberately. He muttered, dropped into the seat behind her. The girl, Marion, went farther back. John Knox took another pull at his Scotch bottle and retired to the very end of the cabin, where he sank down wordlessly.

The pilot crawled into his compartment, shut the door. The starters whirred, the motors coughed and came into action. For a moment or so longer they sat there, revving, speeded up the motors, until at last satisfied, the pilot nosed the plane into the dense fog. It roared over the even ground, lifted its nose and headed into the black murkiness of the thick night.

Every passenger in the plane peered out the windows and tried to make out a landmark, but the fog was too dense. It enveloped them, wrapped itself about them. It was as if they were in another world. Only the steady drone of the twin motors was heard— otherwise nothing earthly. The ship rocked and vibrated like a bus over a rough road.

In the back seat John Knox took another drink, muttered to himself, "I've got to get home, got to see Stella and the kids once more. Then I'll give myself up."

Inez Ashton was saying, "I'll have to think up some emergency to make George give me the money. Jackie will leave me if I don't get him that roadster."

Marion Shipley prayed. "Please, please, let me get to him in time, let me see him just once more before he dies."

Joe Bloom was figuring on the back of an envelope. "A nice profit if Rader takes the stones. I'll set her up in a better apartment then. Sweet kid."

Behind him Soapy was cautioning himself. "Better wait until

we land. It will be foggy and I can sneak a shiv in him and no one the wiser."

The man in the yellow coat clutched his leatherbound package between his knees and glared down over Inez Ashton's shoulder through thick-rimmed glasses. Her dress had fallen away from her white throat. The upper slopes of milk white breasts, generous and redundant, were visible. "Jezebel, Jezebel," muttered the man and gnawed at his moustache.

IN the pilot's compartment the flyer kept his grim eyes fixed on his instruments. His feet and hands caressed the controls with a master's touch. Once he glanced back over his shoulder at his passengers and laughed, but no sound came. His teeth were huge and white, his gums visible, as if he had no lips.

Hours later the big machine still roared its way through the enveloping fog. The only passenger who slept was Bloom. Behind him, Soapy Turco sat grimly waiting, waiting, the knife burning in his armpit. He licked his lips avidly as he thought of those diamonds nestling in the fat one's breast pocket.

The voice of the man in the yellow overcoat startled everyone in the cabin. He grinned with yellowed teeth beneath his ragged moustache, touched Inez Ashton on the shoulder and said, "Are you married, Jezebel?"

A sudden silence in the cabin. Mrs. Ashton smiled, tried to laugh it off.

"Why, yes," she said, "I am."

"I thought so, Jezebel," he half shrieked. "So am I! You remind me of my wife!"

His hand reached down to fumble at her shoulder. She screamed a little and pulled away.

"Let her alone, lug," snarled Soapy, half rising. The man laughed.

"Pardon me, madame. As I said, I too am married. I am returning home now to my wife. Would you like to see the present I am taking her?"

Without waiting for an answer he raised the leather-bound package, clawed at its wrappings, laughing, gurgling all the while. Saliva ran from his thick lips unheeded, drooled over his unshaven chin onto his dirty shirt bosom. "A long distance I went for this present! A long time I searched for it! But I found it and I'm taking it back to her. Look, Jezebel, look!"

INEZ ASHTON screamed. Marion Shipley covered her budding breasts with her hands and cowered back into the corner. John Knox blinked drunkenly, shook his head from side to side as if unwilling to believe his eyes. Bloom and Turco dropped their mouths open in astonishment, gazed with amazement at the gruesome thing in the man's hand. It was a head! A man's head, severed at the neck, held aloft by the clutching fingers of the man in the yellow overcoat. Blood had congealed in deep black clots about the neck stump. The eyes were glaring, the lips stretched taut and tight in a mocking, hideous smile.

"He! he! he!" laughed the man in the yellow overcoat. "My wife's lover. All the way east I sought him and, now that I've found him, I'm taking this back to my wife for a present. Will she like it, Jezebel, Jezebel?"

The rest happened so quick that it was almost unbelievable. The man dropped the head, clutched at the woman. His claw-like fingers darted out, snatched at the neck of her silk dress. There was a ripping sound, the dress tore away, revealing scantily-covered, pendulous, quivering breasts. Her scream echoed above all other noises as the maniac's clutching fingers sank deep into the soft fullness of her shoulder, shaking.

"Jezebel! Jezebel!" he howled.

In the rear of the plane, John Knox rose unsteadily to his feet, poised for a moment and hurled the Scotch bottle. It whizzed by the heads of the struggling pair, crashed against the window and carried the whole pane of glass away. Joe Bloom plunged by Soapy and grabbed the man in the yellow overcoat. John Knox wabbled from the rear of the plane. Marion Shipley screamed frantically as the men rolled and tumbled in the narrow aisle. Soapy Turco shook a blackjack into his hand and went into action. His mind was crafty, working at full speed. In this mixup, he told himself, was a great opportunity.

THE lights went out suddenly. Cautiously Soapy probed the struggling mass beneath him, his thin-bladed knife now in his hand. He made out a stiff collar, a pudgy neck of bulging fat. The knife bit deep, straight downward. Beneath him Joe Bloom groaned and relaxed. A cruel hand snatched the black case from his pocket. The blackjack rose and fell twice, thrice, and the struggling mass was still.

"Turn on the lights!" shrieked Soapy.

The lights came on. The pilot's door was open. Like a huge bug in his goggles and helmet the pilot peered back—and *grinned*. Soapy shuddered at that grin, then was roused by Marion Shipley's scream.

"Stop her, oh, stop her!" shrieked the frantic girl.

Crazed by fright and horror Inez Ashton had clambered through the broken window. Only dimly could her figure be seen on the wing, enveloped by fog, the wind pressing the torn silk of her dress against her mature figure. Breasts free, thighs and hips outlined, she stood there clinging to a strut as the wind slowly tore her tattered outer clothes from her body.

"Come back, come back," roared Soapy and leaped for the window. For a moment he caught a clearer glimpse of her, her face twisted, crazed with horror, blood dripping from cuts on her swaying breasts, cuts from the broken window. Then suddenly the plane swooped, the woman grabbed at another strut, missed and hurtled into the fog.

Thunderstruck Soapy stood like a statue. Then he heard the sobbing of the frightened girl, and above all the thin, reedy laughter of the pilot who still leaned from his enclosure.

"Damn you," howled Soapy, "You threw her off! You did it purposely!" He fought his way toward the enclosure, toward the laughing man who sat at the controls. As he disappeared inside, knife in hand, the girl, Marion Shipley screamed.

"Don't! Don't! We'll all fall."

Inside the pilot's compartment Soapy Turco was cowering back. The faint glow of the dashlight half revealed the flyer. With a careless hand he swept the helmet and goggles from his head, turned to leer at Soapy.

Soapy Turco, hardened killer, murderer of a dozen men, cowered back and whimpered like a frightened child. "No! No!" He fumbled behind him for the door catch, knife in hand.

The pilot grinned more widely than ever. He had no eyes. Only vacant sockets, huge and black. There was no flesh on this skull of his, only bone that gleamed in the half light, teeth that flashed in the bluegummed mouth, wide spread and terrifying.

"No! No!" Soapy moaned again, wide eyed with terror.

THE door clicked open, he stumbled backward over the low sill into the cabin and screamed in agony as he fell, the knife doubled beneath him. The sharp blade that had already tasted blood plunged through the flesh of his back, plunged miraculously between ribs and entered his heart. Soapy fought his way to his feet, coughed once—again—and laid his cheek against the floor while torrents of blood gushed from between his taut lips.

The man at the controls laughed shrilly, put his helmet and goggles back in place. Marion Shipley fainted.

When she regained consciousness, it was as if a voice in her ear said, "Come forward, come forward."

She cringed, tried to make her muscles refuse obedience. Against her will she found herself gaining her feet, stepping over the sprawled bodies in the aisle. Unable to resist she went forward, stepped over the inert body of Soapy Turco and entered the pilot's compartment. She sank into a seat beside the flyer.

In a soft voice he said, "They are dead, dead, all dead."

"Yes," she nodded. Was that her voice?

"They were bad," he continued in his colorless voice, "bad and selfish, animals. You are young, my dear, but Death is just. Because you are good and clean I am taking you to your lover. Sleep, my dear, sleep."

SLEEP seemed to wrap itself about her like the fog. Later she heard his voice at the radio, "Calling Interstate Airways, Chicago, Interstate Airways, Chicago, coming in from the east, coming in from the east; am I on the beam? Am I on the beam?"

A sharp click. Another voice came to her ear, pierced the haze of her sleep. "This is Interstate Airways, Chicago. Who are you and why are you flying? Come on in, you're right on its nose, right on its nose. Who's flying the plane?"

The pilot laughed. "Death is at the controls," he giggled into the mouthpiece.

Down, down, down they zoomed. The girl awakened as the wheels suddenly hit solid earth, as the plane braked and came to a motionless stop.

"Goodbye," said the pilot and opened the door. Without a backward look she plunged from the plane, alit running, and headed into the fog toward the sound of distant voices. She heard the patter of many feet coming toward her, almost fainted as arms reached to help her.

From the thickness of the fog came the roar of an airplane motor, the crunch of rubber tired wheels and the zoom of a heavy plane bounding forward in a takeoff.

THEY hurried her into the lighted office, gave her water, a short drink of whiskey.

"It's Marion Shipley, Mac's sweetheart!"

"Who flew you in, Miss Shipley, and why did he leave? Who was it?"

The girl struggled to a sitting posture. "Get me a cab," she gasped. "Who flew me in? Death or the devil! It doesn't matter!"

Hours later at the hospital she sat with an arm beneath young McAfee's head, clutching his fingers with her own. Wordlessly she sat there while from a bureau a radio spoke softly.

"News flash: The missing plane Nc-1645, property of the Interstate Airways of Pittsburg, has been found. It crashed eighteen miles southwest of Chicago at midnight last night, resulting in the deaths of all on board. Fire consumed the ship. None of the bodies have been positively identified but authorities hope to complete identification soon. The pilot is thought to have bailed out, deserting the ship when it got out of control, for the three bodies found were clothed in civilian clothes. No one knows who the pilot was, the thief who stole the plane, but authorities expect to locate him at an early hour today."

Marion Shipley leaned and kissed the warm lips of the man she loved.

THE SECRET OF OLD FARM

They were going to be happy, Hal thought when he married
the girl. For how could that simple little scar of hers transform
her life into a nightmare? There were dark matters that
Hal didn't understand, and there was the grim old woman's
words: "God's curse on you both—she's not for marriage!"

*H*AL WINTHROP *had* been prepared for expostulation, even for anger, but he hadn't foreseen that look of terror on Doris Wayne's face when she opened the door of the century-old New England farmhouse and saw him.

"You here, Hal? Oh, God!" She burst into frantic sobbing. "Go away! How dared you come here? Didn't I tell you I could never see you again?"

Hal took her hands from her face, drew her to him, feeling the warmth of her rounded breasts against him. "I came because I can't live without you, Doris," he answered. "You left me just because we had come to care for each other during that year you worked in my office. I know that there's some mystery in your life. Tell me what it is, darling, because I'm going to marry you today. Yes, I've made all the arrangements."

"Today?" That cry was of despair, utter and hopeless. "You're mad Hal. I told you—"

A high-pitched cackle from within interrupted her. An aged, blear-eyed crone came hobbling out of the parlor, followed by a grim-faced woman of middle age. Doris tried to detain her, but the old creature dodged adroitly, and came sidling up to Hal, glancing at him with a look of pathetic coquetry.

"Go away, Dorry! This is my beau!" she cackled. "Ain't you ashamed of yourself, stealing my beaux away from me?"

"Granny, dear, go back and be quiet," pleaded Doris. "Mrs. Campion, take her to the parlor."

The grim-faced woman led the old creature away, after giving Hal a look of malevolence. It was evident that she had overheard his speech to Doris. The girl turned to him again.

"There! Now you know the truth!" she said. "My grandmother's demented and has to be taken care of like a baby. Is that reason enough for you?"

"No reason at all," said Hal. "I'm willing to assume the charge of her."

"I tell you it can't be!" cried Doris.

But Hal's arms were about her, and long, shuddering sighs shook her as she vainly sought to avoid his lips.

"You love me, darling. Nothing else matters," he pleaded.

"There's—there's something more. I—I'm scarred. I had an operation on my hip when I was a child. You'll hate me for it."

Hal laughed. "I'm going to marry you," he answered, "and take that dreadful scar on trust. The preacher's waiting for us at Hambledon. You're coming with me now!"

The door opened again, and the grim-faced Mrs. Campion looked out. "You can't marry her," she said, each word cold and precise as a hammer-blow. "Best go back where you come from."

"I'm marrying you now," said Hal to Doris.

IT was over, and they two were coming out of the parsonage at Hambledon, man and wife, Doris on Hal's arm. He put her into the seat in his coupé and started back. Doris lay with her cheek against Hal's, sobbing, sobbing.

Hal patted her hand. "Darling, you're overwrought," he said. "I shouldn't have taken you by surprise this way, but I knew it was the only way I'd ever get you."

"Oh Hal, I love you, and I shouldn't have been so weak! Oh, I don't know what to do!"

"Is it your grandmother, dearest? Or are you worrying about that scar? You foolish child, as if that's going to make any difference!"

But Doris went on sobbing dismally, hopelessly, and only tried to dry her eyes when the car stopped in front of the farm-house.

An ancient, gloomy place, Hal thought. It was built entirely of

*"Go back, Hal! For
God's sake, go back!"
Doris screamed.*

native stone. By day it had seemed gloomy enough, but now, in
the dusk, with its many shuttered windows, and the great stone
foundations, it seemed to have acquired some sinister quality, as
if the dead generations who had inhabited it had imbued it with
some secret and mysterious memories of evil.

Just for an instant Hal had the illusion that he saw Doris's face
at a lower window. Doris's face, and yet the face of a fiend, so
twisted with evil and malignant passion. There was the hate and
sorrow of a lost soul in that distorted countenance.

So real did it seem, that Hal uttered a cry and started forward.
And then the vision was gone, and he knew that it had been only
his imagination at play.

Angry because he was letting his wife's fears affect him, Hal
drove the car into the big, empty barn, and went back to the house.

It was gloomier inside than without. The oil lamps shed long shadows across the great room, in which Mrs. Campion was laying the table. It was filled with the massive furniture of a century ago. And Doris was not there. The woman glanced at Hal with the same hostile and malignant look.

"I hope we're all going to get on well together," Hal ventured.

"You're a fool," she answered. "And a fool pays for his folly. Don't forget that. She should have sent you away."

"Why?" Hal demanded. "Why don't you approve of Doris marrying me?"

"God's curse is on you both," snarled the grim woman. "She ain't for marriage. Oh, you'll learn. You'll learn." She moved quickly away as Doris came into the room.

"*BUT* you mustn't hide it from me, darling, just to ease your own mind." And Hal raised the garment and looked at the scar. "Why, how absurd, sweetheart!" he exclaimed. "Did you suppose I'd love you less because of that?"

"I ought to kill you!" said Hal. His blow caught the doctor on the jaw.

"It's a disfigurement! I'm unclean, unclean!" cried the girl wildly.

Hal drew her into his arms and kissed her until she returned his kisses. It was certainly a bad scar. It ran from the point of the thigh upward, over the hip, and ended in the hollow of the waist. But it wasn't even a disfigurement, and there was nothing repulsive about it.

Certainly it didn't worry Hal. How could it, when he had Doris for his very own. That slender form, so pliant in his arms.

Hal kneeled before her in worship and kissed her hands. "Darling, I want you always to understand how much I love you," he told her.

And later, when he held her in his arms and felt her lips against his own, and the warm pressure of her young breasts, with the heart throbbing in unison with his own beneath them—then Hal thought that Doris had forgotten those inhibitions of hers.

"We're going to be happy, aren't we, dearest?" Hal whispered drowsily.

And he fell asleep, knowing that in the morning everything would be straightened out, especially the matter of granny. If there was anything besides granny and that ridiculous scar, Doris would tell him then. And then he would have all their lives in which to make her happy.

THE next thing of which Hal was aware was that wild peal of maniacal laughter coming from somewhere—somewhere beneath the room in which he slept.

He started up, and it sounded again, far off and muffled, but shrill, vibrant, demoniacal.

And Hal realized that Doris was no longer beside him.

Mad with fear, he leaped to his feet, thrust on his shoes, and rushed into the corridor, shouting Doris's name.

From somewhere underneath came a gibbering babble. Hal raced down the stairs, groping through the dark rooms on the ground floor. He ran through the dining-room and kitchen, seeking the entrance to the cellar, from which that sound seemed to have come, stumbling over chairs, and bruising himself against the edges of tables.

"Doris! Doris!" he shouted.

Again he heard that burst of maniacal laughter, but faint and smothered underneath. Then, as he groped wildly for the cellar stairs, a white-clad form appeared, and two arms were flung about him.

It was Mrs. Campion, in her nightdress, and the embrace was anything but affectionate. It was effectual in its restraint, and there were hints of a knowledge of jiu-jitsu in the way in which the woman adroitly seized Hal's arm and locked it.

"Stay where you are, Mr. Winthrop! Everything will be all right!"

"Doris! Where's Doris?" shouted Hal.

"Here, Hal, here!" Doris appeared, a slighter figure, her bare feet padding on the linoleum of the kitchen floor. "I'm all right, darling. But granny—poor granny—she's fallen down the cellar stairs. Hal, you've got to drive into Litchfield and get Dr. Baynes. Will you go at once?"

Hall breathed a deep sigh of relief. "You had me scared almost to death," he answered shakily. "I'll go at once. That was your grandmother laughing?"

"Yes, yes, yes," Doris whispered.

"I'll carry her up."

"No," said Mrs. Campion. "I'll attend to her. You drive into Litchfield. You passed it on the way here. It's only nine miles."

Hal was in no mood for controversy. "I'll go," he said.

HIS car ate up the miles. A solitary policeman on patrol directed him to Baynes' house. Baynes came to the door in his pajamas, with a dressing-gown thrown about him, at Hal's ring.

Under the light in the hall Hal saw a youngish man, not over forty, at any rate, with a somewhat dissipated look and furtive eyes.

"My wife's grandmother's fallen down the cellar steps and hurt herself," Hal explained. "At Old Farm."

"Your wife's!" exclaimed Baynes.

"I married Doris Wayne at Hambledon this afternoon. She had been my office assistant in Boston. We'd been—well, engaged."

"You fool!" snapped Baynes.

"Thanks for the compliment," said Hal, "but we'll leave out personalities. I guess I'm not going to like you any better than you like me. But Mrs. Campion asked me to drive in and bring you back."

For an instant Baynes' dark eyes regarded Hal with that furtive glance of his. It was plain to Hal that Baynes had been badly disturbed by the news of the marriage.

"I'll come," Baynes snapped. "I'll be ready in five minutes. I'll drive my own car. You can drive back, Mr. Winthrop. I'll be there as soon as you are."

But, as Hal was turning to the door, Baynes halted him with a peremptory, "Wait! How many of you are there at Old Farm?"

"Why, there's my wife and myself, her grandmother, and Mrs. Campion," answered Hal, nettled still more by the doctor's manner. "Did you think we were entertaining a wedding party?"

Baynes made no answer. He turned away, a sneer upon his lips, and Hal went out.

"I think, my friend, that a good punch to the jaw would do you a world of good," he reflected, as he got into his car.

BAYNES didn't keep his promise to be at Old Farm as soon as Hal, for Hal drove his speedometer up to sixty-five on the return journey. He felt his fears increasing as he drove. He didn't quite know what it was he feared, but he knew Doris and Mrs. Campion were keeping something from him—something that Baynes had guessed at.

He leaped out of his car and ran into the house. The oil lamp was burning in the parlor. And Hal had a prescience of evil even before he burst into the room.

Even before he eluded the clutching arm of Mrs. Campion, as she tried to bar his way, he saw the inanimate figure of the old woman on the old-fashioned sofa, with Doris kneeling at her side, swabbing, swabbing with a blood-stained rag. Why, this was death!

Death in the air, like something tangible. Death in the haggard face that Doris turned upon Hal. Death on the features of the old, demented woman, now become so strangely placid, and even dignified.

"Hal, go away! Don't look! Don't come here, Hal!" screamed Doris, trying to interpose herself before the body, to screen it from Hal's eyes.

But Hal had seen. The old woman lay almost nude on the sofa, and there was a ghastly knife-wound ripping up the entire body, from the shrunken breasts to the waist. And there was blood everywhere, blood that Doris had been vainly trying to wipe away.

Blood, too, staining the hands of the grim-faced woman who came toward Hal.

"Yes, you may as well know the truth," she said. "Mrs. Emmett killed herself with a kitchen knife. She was a homicidal maniac, and I was here to take care of her. She was too crafty for me. Now you know everything."

Hal caught the furtive glances that she and Doris exchanged. Then there sounded the purr of Baynes' motor car outside. Baynes came into the room.

BUT did Hal know everything?

The secret had been well kept, and Baynes wrote out a certificate of death by apoplexy. The funeral was over. Days were passing. With Doris in a state of nervous breakdown, there was little that Hal could do, save watch over her.

Had Mrs. Emmett really slashed herself to death in that inhuman way, or…?

What was the secret held by the grim woman who stalked through the house, assiduous in her attendance upon Doris, but coldly hostile toward Hal?

That was a point at which Hal's mind faltered. He could only watch and wait. Some hell's broth was brewing, and he had always known nothing but evil could come out of the ancient, desolate farmhouse that held so many secrets of the dead generations.

"Darling, you've got to listen to me," Hal protested. "I'm going to take you away. To Boston, where you'll be able to forget. There's nothing to hold you here now."

Hal had said that a dozen times, and each time Doris had gone into hysterics. This time she was strangely calm.

"Hal, I'm not going away," she answered. "This is my home. Hal, I ran away from you, and you followed me here. You made me marry you. It was a mistake, a tragic error. I don't blame you, Hal, poor Hal. But—but—I want you to go away and leave me. There can be no happiness for us ever."

Hal remembered the grim woman's words, "God's curse is on you both. She's not for marriage."

He took his wife's hands in his. "Doris, my sweet, tell me if there's something I haven't been told. What is it, dear, what is it?

"I know that Mrs. Campion has been a hospital nurse. I can guess she's been used to handling insane patients. Dear, there's nothing you can't tell me. If you—oh, Doris, if you're one of those people who have periodical attacks of dementia—forgive me for suggesting it—you can still trust me. Tell me why you've got to stay here, why we can't go away for ever."

Hal was thinking of that ghastly, distorted face of Doris that he had imagined he had seen at the window. Had it been imagination?

She burst into wild, shrill laughter. "I'm sane," she cried. "I'm sane. Too sane to keep up this dreadful farce. Leave me to go to hell in my own way."

"I'll let you go to hell in your own way," said Hal, "but I'll never leave you."

SHE left his side at night. Hal knew that now, and a certain loyalty forbade him to follow her. He guessed it was for the purpose of talking to Mrs. Campion. He guessed that Doris in spite of her denials, suffered from periodical attacks of insanity. And somehow Hal had come to place his faith in that grim attendant, despite her sullen and malignant hostility toward him.

Twice during the week, three times during the next week, Hal awoke in the night to find his wife gone from his side, and feigning sleep, waited until she stole back beside him before the dawn. Two or three times Hal had thought that he heard the sound of a distant motor car. But it wasn't until he was sure that a car was parked somewhere near the house that he followed Doris.

Softly down the stairs. Softly into the unlit parlor. Softly, pausing at the door, until he heard Doris sobbing hysterically. Then he opened the door quietly, and saw her, faintly silhouetted within, and the man beside her, with his hand upon her shoulder. Baynes! By God, Baynes, with his dissipated face! Baynes, making love by night to Doris, after she had stolen from his side to meet him!

Hal leaped forward, a torrent of invective breaking from his lips. His blow caught the doctor upon the jaw and sent him reeling.

"Winthrop, you damn' fool! Winthrop!" shouted Baynes.

Hal suddenly grew cool as ice. "I ought to kill you, you damn' swine," he said. "If you've got to make love to my wife, you might do it decently in the daytime, not when she steals out at night to meet you!"

Doris's hands dropped on Hal's shoulders. "Hal, what are you saying?" she cried. "Oh God, you don't believe that of me, do you?"

"I'm no man's fool, nor no woman's either. What else is he here for? Why else have you been meeting him, night after night? Did you think I was asleep? Did you suppose I didn't know?"

"Hal, you're crazy! He—he came to treat me. My nerves! I'm overwrought. I—"

"No need to lie!" Hal rasped. He turned to Baynes. "Get out of this house!" he said. "Make love to my wife like a man, not like a dog. If I find you here again, I'll kill you!"

EVERYTHING went quietly the next day. Mrs. Campion knew—Hal was convinced of that. He knew that she had been watching those love trysts of Baynes and Doris. Oh, there was a lot that Hal didn't yet know, but he knew that Baynes was his wife's lover.

He guessed that Doris, if not insane, suffered from some mental disorder that rendered her irresponsible, and that Mrs. Campion was staying in the house to look after her. And the thought that Baynes would take advantage of a crazy girl was goading Hal to the point of madness.

He meant to kill Baynes for the dog he was. He was making up his mind the following night, as he lay in his bed across the hall from Doris's room. He had moved there, because he couldn't profane that relationship of marriage any more. He was thinking hard. If he killed Baynes, that was the end. If he didn't he must take Doris away, force her to come with him, as he had forced her to the altar.

He wished that he had killed Baynes. Perhaps, on the morrow....

Doris hadn't spoken a word to him that day, but Hal had seen madness in her eyes. And Mrs. Campion, going so stealthily about her work....

Hal was thinking all this, between sleep and wakefulness, when the mind is most active, yet wraps an element of illusion about its processes. Suddenly Hal realized that he was very tired, that the strain of the past days had driven him down, down into the same nebulous state of mind as Doris's. He only wanted to sleep now, to rest and, for the while, forget.

Then suddenly the scream of agony, and again that mad burst of demoniac laughter. Laughter horrible, unhuman, as a damned soul might laugh from the pit of hell. And Hal had thought that it had been the old, dead woman who had laughed before!

He was upon his feet. He was in Doris's room. But Doris wasn't there!

Scream after scream, dying away in pain-racked agony! Screams coming from Mrs. Campion's room at the end of the hall!

As Hal ran toward it, he heard again that demoniac laughter, coming from somewhere beneath him.

He burst into Mrs. Campion's room. The blaze of moonlight, coming through the open window, showed Mrs. Campion, writhing on the bed in her death agony. Her nightdress had been slit from top to bottom, and her body had been ripped in the same way as Mrs. Emmett's. She had been horribly cut up and from that mutilated body the black blood was dripping, dripping to the floor.

Even as Hal reached her side, the death-rattle sounded in her throat. She quivered and lay still.

Hal knew now. Knew who had killed her, and Mrs. Emmett too. The girl who had been so gentle, so efficient in his Boston office. Doris, his wife!

ONCE more, but faintly, that peal of devilish laughter sounded from the cellar. Hal left the side of the dead woman and went downstairs. His brain was cool as ice. God, what a fool he had been not to have understood before!

He was going to take the madwoman away, to flee with her through the night. His wife, and Baynes's mistress! No matter!

His wife, whom he had sworn to love and honor! He was going to stand by her and protect her.

Very softly Hal went down the cellar steps. He had been down before, and seen the barred door which, Doris told him, led to the old well. Hal guessed that the door would be open now, and he didn't believe in that well any longer. He knew he'd find his wife behind that door.

Just as he surmised, the door was open, but all behind it was pitch darkness. Yet out of that darkness came a soft, melodious sound, as of a woman crooning over a child, or lover.

Hal stepped through the entrance. "Doris!" he called. "Doris, come to me, dear!"

At once the crooning ceased, but there came no answer. And, now the darkness seemed to be shot through with infinite evil. All the unseen powers of hell seemed to lurk in that darkness, waiting, waiting malignantly to destroy Hal, and Doris, too.

Hal stood still. "Doris, my dear, come to me!" he called again. "Come here, my sweet! I'm not going to harm you!"

He heard a stealthy movement near him, and turned in that direction, his arms outstretched. "Come to me, dear!" he called and caught his breath in a sob.

Another peal of maniacal laughter answered him, so near that the vibrations jarred his ear-drums. And, even in that dense darkness, Hal seemed to visualize it. Something dwarfish—and not Doris. Something like a fiend materialized out of the pit of hell.

"Go back! For God's sake go back, Hal!" came Doris's scream. And that was not the high-pitched note of the laughing maniac.

A violent blow in the groin doubled Hal up in agony. Then something dropped upon his head, hard, heavy, filling the world with lambent light. And consciousness dissolved.

LIGHT gleamed in Hal's eyes. He hadn't been out long, hadn't really been out at all. All through that brief period of unconsciousness his mind had been at work, weaving fantasies, hellish fantasies in which he had been battling with Doris, a screaming maniac, to keep her from killing herself by ripping up her lovely body with the knife.

Now Hal came back to himself suddenly, to find himself extended on his back in the cellar, bound with ropes, so that he was unable to move hand or foot. Near him, in the light of the oil lamp, Doris lay, similarly bound.

Her night attire had been torn to tatters, and she lay, the picture of beauty, with her small breasts flattened against her chest, the long, tapering limbs and slender wrists and ankles.

And, crouching over Doris, almost fingering the scar upon her hip, was something that seared Hal's soul with horror.

It had the face of Doris, save for the look of frightful malevolent triumph. But it wasn't Doris. It was a male dwarf—less than a dwarf, a homuncule, not more than two feet high. A man, and yet the tiny embryo of a man that had no right to exist upon God's earth. A tiny creature, and yet perfectly formed, nude, save for a rag about its loins, with rippling muscles bulging on the chest, and stunted arms and legs. The chest and face were hairless.

Hal screamed with horror, and the tiny creature looked up and picked up a long knife that lay beside it.

"He-he-he-he-he-he!" it roared, filling the cellar with that same maniacal laughter. "Your turn's come, Hal Winthrop. I've killed the rest of them, because I'm going to be alone with her. So your turn's come. Maybe I'll kill her and myself too, afterward, because we belong together. My blood in her, her blood in me, destined for each other to all eternity!"

"Will, darling, listen!" Doris pleaded. "I love Hal, and he hasn't done you any harm. Don't kill him!"

"No harm?" piped the tiny thing in its shrill voice. "They've kept me here in the dark ever since you came, for fear you'd find me, but I've been watching both of you. I dug a hole out of this place, and nobody guessed it, and I got ropes and the knife. I killed the old woman first, and then the other one, and now I'm going to kill you, so that Doris and I can be together.

"You didn't have to come here, you fool, you fool! They shut me up when you came. Before that, I was free. Now I'm sending you to hell. To hell, do you understand?"

"**WILL,** darling! Will!" screamed Doris. "I tell you he means you no harm. Let him go, Will. Do anything you like to me, but let him go. He'll promise to go away and never come here again!"

But suddenly the tiny creature seemed to go mad with frenzy. Curses drooled from its lips, as it leaped up and down, the knife gripped tightly in the tiny fist, a kitchen knife, thin, flexible, and worn down to a ribbon-edge of steel.

"I'm going to kill you slow, Winthrop," it shrieked. "You've seen her scar, damn you. My scar—do you hear? My scar! I'm going to cut you into pieces slow, Winthrop!"

Suddenly the little monster leaped upon Hal's body and made a vicious slash at his arm. Hal felt the keen edge of the knife, as it bit into the flesh, and the spurt of blood that followed. Doris shrieked again, and struggled in her ropes.

"Will, for God's sake have pity!"

The monster sprang from Hal's body and turned toward her, as if momentarily undecided what to do next. And in that instant Hal made a discovery that gave him hope.

The edge of the blade, that had made the gash across his arm, had all but severed the cord that bound that arm to his body. Only a single wrench, and he could free it. If he could entice the monster within grasp of his hand....

It crouched there, brooding, muttering, gathering its insane will for the next act. Hal was to remember afterward the oddness of that silence, with Doris lying struggling in her ropes, and himself measuring the monster's probable leap.

Then, with an ear-splitting peal of insane laughter, it leaped again. It landed on Hal's stomach, just as he had forecast. The knife was raised to slash his throat.

With a single, violent wrench, Hal broke the rope that fastened his right wrist, and seized the tiny thing by one leg, raising it on high.

It screeched maniacally, and slashed at Hal's arm, bringing the knife-edge across it again before Hal had raised it out of reach. With all his strength he held it there, prepared to dash it to the ground and stun it, while it curled and writhed and screamed in fury.

"Why, how absurd," Hal exclaimed. "Did you suppose I'd love you less because of that scar?"

Higher still Hal raised it, while Doris screamed, and then suddenly went off in a dead faint.

Higher and higher, while obscene venom drooled from the creature's lips, and it made frantic passes with the knife.

Suddenly the roar of an automatic sounded through the cellar. And now it was a faceless thing that Hal was holding, a crimson horror spattering him with its blood.

The writhing ceased, and, as Hal's hand relaxed its hold, the monster dropped to the ground beside him, dead.

A man came striding into the cellar. Hal recognized Dr. Baynes, the still smoking automatic in his hands.

"God!" cried Baynes. "I had to do it, Doris. I told you I'd hold off as long as possible. I had to do it. He'd have killed you both!"

IN the bedroom Hal sat beside his sleeping wife. Baynes faced him gravely. That furtive look was gone from his eyes, and Hal realized that he had misjudged him.

"Will was Doris's twin brother," Baynes explained. "The children had crowded each other before birth, and Doris had become a normal infant, leaving Will a tiny, shriveled thing. That was why she had always felt that sense of deep responsibility toward him. That was what he meant by their having the same blood in their veins.

"He worshipped her. She was the only person who could handle him, for he was warped mentally from birth, and his experience of life didn't improve him any. It was only lately that he developed homicidal tendencies.

"I had made Doris go to Boston and take a position, feeling that she was in danger of losing her sanity by living solely for Will.

"When I came here to see Doris at night, it was because we were trying to devise some means of getting him away secretly. She was desperately afraid you would find out about Will, and leave her, and she told me she was madly in love with you.

"I told her, after he killed their grandmother, that none of you were safe, but we didn't guess that he had dug a way out of the cellar, and was able to prowl about the house at night.

"I told, Doris, if the worst came to the worst, that I should have to shoot him, and that I should be on the watch every night in case the opportunity came of getting him secretly away. I came tonight, just in time to save you both.

"You thought, naturally, that I was in love with your wife. I am, and have always been, Winthrop, but she has never looked on me as anything but a friend, and with that I have had to be content."

"But her scar—her scar?" asked Hal.

Baynes hesitated. "I suppose I'll have to tell you, Winthrop," he answered. "The twins were born united at the hip. My father separated them. Generally such operations are fatal to one or the other. But both survived. You see now? You understand? God bless you both!"

He gripped Hal's hand and strode out of the room.

Hal looked down at Doris, sleeping peacefully under the influence of the injection that Baynes had given her, and thanked God that the secret of Old Farm was solved for ever.

JEROME SEVERS PERRY

"I MUST HAVE 5 CORPSES"

No women of the streets would do if he were
to save the wife he loved more than life itself.
He must murder five young, innocent girls!

*T**HIS MUST** not* happen, Dent Traynor told himself. This could not happen. Lola was too young to die. Lola was too sweet and too lovely to die. Dent loved her too much to let her die.

Bare-headed, coatless, he wandered through the night's drenching rain, feeling no cold and oblivious to the soaking downpour that plastered his shirt to his muscular shoulders and deep, thick chest. Lola must not die, he kept repeating to himself, over and over like a cracked phonograph record. *Lola must not die!*

He clenched his fists until the nails dug blood from his palms. And as he went forward through the storm, he thought of his lovely golden-haired Lola; his sweet bride, Lola; his life, and his heart, and his love.

She was all these things to Traynor. She was his soul, his existence. Without her he would not care to live. Without her the world would be a bitter place of haunting, poignant emptiness.

Lola must not die!

Only five days ago she had been joyously gay, full of the sweet zest of youth and health and happiness. And now....

Dent thought of her, lying upon her pillow in the pallid shadows of approaching dissolution. He thought of her white, bloodless face and her small, firm breasts that rose and fell so imperceptibly that almost it seemed that she did not breathe at all. This was not his Lola of the lilting voice and ardent passion. This was not his Lola of the warm arms and vibrant body. This was another Lola, silent and still and bloodless in the Valley of the Shadow. This was another Lola, whose violet eyes were closed and whose heart beat faintly as Death's dark fingers brushed her, summoned her....

She must not die, Dent Traynor whispered bitterly. And so, in the rain and in the midnight, he came at last to the house he had been seeking.

IT was a dark and somber dwelling, lurking in the blackness of a small, mean street. And over it there seemed to hover an atmosphere of occult evil, an aura of strange dread that struck ominously at Traynor's consciousness. But he fought down the fear that assailed him; throttled the shudder that quivered his flesh. What did it matter if this house was evil? Dent would have gone willingly into the slimy jaws of hell itself, if it meant that his beloved Lola would live again....

He knocked upon the door.

The portal opened, and Dent stared into slanted, glittering eyes set in a face of wrinkled yellow parchment. It was the face of a demon, he thought at first. The evil face of a devil from the nethermost pits. There was slithering malignity in those glittering, slanted eyes. There was sardonic, inhuman diabolism in the thin, unsmiling mouth.

Yet Traynor was unafraid. He forced himself to be unafraid. In that evil, hairless skull reposed a brain crawling with forbidden knowledge; and out of that crawling knowledge might come a cure for his beloved Lola....

Dent spoke. "You are Dr. Wu Chang?"

The wrinkled Chinese bowed. "I am Wu Chang. And you, of course, are Dent Traynor."

Traynor stiffened. "How did you know my name?"

Wu Chang grinned, displaying toothless gums of vivid, blood-crimson hue. "I know all things," he said in his voice that was like the crackling of dried parchment. "Enter, and tell me what you seek of me."

Dent Traynor stepped over the threshold of the Chinese doctor's house.

And as he entered, a violent revulsion seized upon his soul, for the place reeked of nameless, slithering evil things beyond the ken of ordinary mortals. The very atmosphere of the house seemed permeated with hellish malevolence. It was in the incense that drifted noxiously in little blue wisps before Dent's eyes. It was in the dark shadows that lurked thirstily in the far corners. Evil! Evil! Evil!

IN his long yellow robes decorated with silken purple dragons, Wu Chang stood immobile at the room's center, under a greenish, sickly light that outlined the demoniac quality of his wrinkled features. "Speak, Dent Traynor," the Chinese physician whispered in his ghost's voice. "Speak, and tell me what you seek of me."

"I seek a cure for my wife!" Traynor cried out from the depths of his tortured heart.

As he shot, Cherry Blossom leaped into his line of fire.

"Your wife is ill?"

"Yes! Ill with a strange illness. I have had many doctors for her since she fell sick four days ago. None are able to diagnose the cause of her condition. She lies in a coma, and the blood seemed drained from her veins. They tell me she's dying...." Dent choked in his throat. Then, raspingly, he cried: "She must not die! She cannot die!"

"You love her very much?"

"More than my own life!"

"And what are you willing to pay me?"

"I'll mortgage my life, my future, to you. I haven't much cash—only a few thousand dollars—but you can have it all. You can have anything—"

"I think it can be arranged," Wu Chang smiled evilly. Then, "How did you happen to come to me?"

"We have a new Chinese maid," Traynor said. "She told me of you. She spoke of your magic."

"It is well. Come; take me to your wife." The Chinese plucked at Traynor's arm; and at the touch of the old man's skinny, claw-like, skeletal fingers, Traynor felt a cold, maggoty shudder traversing his flesh.

Together they left the house; went out into the lancing rain that daggered out of the somber, lowering clouds. To Traynor, the next fifteen minutes were as nothing. Almost magically he found himself at his own front door; how he had reached his home, he did not know. He had no recollection of walking the distance….

Wu Chang was still beside him. Traynor unlocked the door, took the sinister old man inside. Led him to the room where Lola lay in white-faced, pallid stillness.

Wu Chang stared down at the unconscious, yellow-haired girl. She was lovely with an ethereal beauty; a beauty both of the flesh and of the spirit. Her eyes were closed, and her breathing was so faint that almost it could not be detected.

Slowly, the Chinese drew down the covers from Lola Traynor's form. His skeletal hands went out, pulled her thin silken night-robe down over her motionless shoulders until he had bared her to the waist.

TRAYNOR would have protested; for Wu Chang's evil eyes were glittering as they feasted upon the rounded enticements of Lola's nude breasts. And the wicked old man's very gaze seemed a profanation, a defilement.

But when Traynor opened his lips to voice his protest, he felt a touch upon his arm. He turned, and saw Cherry-Blossom, his wife's young Chinese maid, looking at him with an odd light of fear in her mysterious, slanted eyes.

"Do not interfere with Wu Chang, O my master!" she whispered. "Remember, he is your only hope of saving the life of my mistress, your wife."

And so Traynor remained silent, choking back his rising gorge as he saw the ancient Asiatic touch Lola's fair white skin lightly. There was something desecrating, in the way Wu Chang's gnarled fingers sank into that pliant, satiny flesh. The old man seemed to be cataloguing her nubility, weighing her loveliness, measuring her capacity for love....

At last, with seeming reluctance, Wu Chang withdrew his probing fingers. He turned to Traynor. "She must be removed to my house at once. And then I will tell you what must be done to save her."

Dent shivered at the chill, ophidian gleam in the Asiatic's glittering eyes. He shuddered at the oily, worm-like evil in Wu Chang's sinister voice. "No!" Traynor whispered hoarsely. "She can't be moved to your house in this rain! Already she's at the verge of death—!"

"To save her, you must bring her to my house!" Wu Chang intoned in a voice of inflexible command.

"But—"

"I promise you she will not die of the exposure."

"You—you're sure?"

"I am positive."

Dent Traynor's will recoiled from the more powerful will of Wu Chang. His shoulders slumped. The thought of taking his beloved, golden-haired Lola to the evil Asiatic's house brought a revulsion to his soul; but he knew there was no other way. To save her, he must obey Wu Chang in all things....

"Very well," he whispered.

And so, with the aid of the Chinese maid, Cherry-Blossom, the limp and unconscious figure of Lola was bundled and swathed in heavy blankets, carried out into the storm-lacerated night. And again Traynor had no remembrance of the time that passed until he was once more under Wu Chang's roof.

AND at last the lovely Lola was safely in a bed in an upper room of Wu Chang's house; and the Chinese drew Traynor back downstairs. "I would talk with you, Dent Traynor," he said slowly. "I would tell you what is needed to restore your wife to health."

"Anything! Anything that's necessary!" Traynor rasped. "Tell me what is needed, and I'll do it!"

"You are quite sure that you would stop at nothing?" the old man asked in a curious, flat tone.

"I tell you, I love Lola more than life itself! I'll do anything you ask of me!"

"You would even risk your soul?"

"Yes! Before God, yes."

"Then listen closely to me, Dent Traynor. To save Lola, your wife, *I must have five corpses!*"

"Five corpses? Good God—!"

"Yes. Five corpses. Five fresh corpses. The bodies of five young girls newly dead."

"You—you want me to rob some graveyard—?"

"No. I want you to *murder five young women!*" Wu Chang smiled his toothless, demoniac smile.

Traynor's belly churned; the vomit of horror arose in his throat, bitterly, like gall and wormwood. He staggered. His knees buckled under him at the impact of Wu Chang's evil words. "You—you want me to… kill… five… girls…?"

"Yes, Dent Traynor. And it must be done tonight. At once. Else your wife will surely die; for nothing can save her except the black sorcery which I alone possess. And that magic cannot be employed unless I have the coagulating blood from the veins of five young women freshly killed."

Traynor's reason reeled; his immortal soul peered into a black maw of hell which opened before him. Five women—the blood of five young girls—five lives which he must take with his own hand, in order to save the life of his lovely, beloved Lola…!

And then his love conquered his revulsion and his horror. He knew that he would barter his chance of immortality for the life

The girl screamed once.
Then he was upon her.

of the golden-haired woman who was his bride. And so he met Wu Chang's dark, basilisk-like eyes. "I—I'll do it!" he grated between clenched teeth. And again his nails bit blood from his palms.

Wu Chang nodded. "Yes. I knew you would. Now attend me. I shall give you a bottle of some strange and potent poison. You will go out into the night, in search of your victims. At the proper moment, you will saturate a handkerchief with some of the stuff from this bottle; you will hold the handkerchief to the nostrils of the girl you have chosen. When she becomes unconscious, you will bring her here to me; then you will go out for still another victim, until you have brought me five girls."

"And then—?" Traynor whispered.

"And then the five girls will die. Slowly, and peacefully, without pain. They will die as the drug takes effect upon their veins, their hearts. And when they are dead, we will use their blood for the black magic which is to cure your wife."

"I… I understand…" Traynor muttered, sickened.

"And remember one thing!" Wu Chang warned. "The girls must be young; they must be beautiful."

"Yes. I… understand…" Dent Traynor said again.

AND then he had the bottle of colorless liquid which the evil Asiatic gave to him; and he found himself once more out in the rain-swept night.

A long while he wandered, aimlessly and dully. And then, abruptly, his heart leaped with a black triumph. He saw a girl standing under the shelter of an awning; a girl thinly clad, dark of hair, slender of form. A girl of the night; shabbily and gar-ishly clad, wearing too much rouge and too much lipstick.

Her tired, worldly eyes fell upon Traynor as he approached her. She smiled an evil smile, inviting and challenging and bold. And she arched out her breasts through her thin, rain-soaked dress, so that he could perceive the globe-like, pouting roundness of them. Her hips swayed a little. She smiled again.

Traynor went up to her. "Hello," he said. His voice was thick in his throat.

"Hello, big boy," she answered him with professional coquetry. "Wet night, ain't it?"

"Very wet."

"I hate the rain, don't you?" she said.

"Yes. I hate the rain."

"Well, then, why don't we do something about it? I got a place near here. Would you like to come up and get acquainted, maybe?" she made no pretense of masking her profession.

"Yes. I'd like to go with you," Dent whispered.

She took his arm. "Then let's go!"

She led him to a doorway nearby; took him upstairs to a dingy, shoddy room. She unfastened her wet frock and peeled herself out of it.

Dent Traynor saw that she wore no brassiere; wore, in fact,

nothing beneath the dress except cheap rayon step-ins that clung intimately to her lush lips…. Her slightly pendulous breasts were white and cream-smooth and inviting… matching the invitation in her hard, weary eyes….

"Kiss me, big boy!" she commanded.

He went to her and kissed her, hating himself for that Judas-caress; hating his mouth that welded upon her lips, hating his arms that simulated the embrace of love.

But he must go through with it, he told himself. He must, for the sake of Lola. And so he made love as the street-girl expected him to; and when at last she murmured sleepily in simulation of utter weariness, he furtively uncorked the vial which Wu Chang had given him. He poured some of the colorless liquid upon a handkerchief; pressed it against his feminine victim's face—

Her struggles were brief, frantic, useless. As the pungent, chloroform-like liquid seeped into her consciousness she grew limp, senseless. Her eyes closed. She lay as one dead….

DENT TAYLOR wrapped her in a blanket, put out the room's single blowsy light. Then he carried the brunette girl down to the street; and, seeking the dark, unfrequented alleys, he brought her to Wu Chang's sinister house.

"What is this!" Wu Chang snarled harshly when he beheld the girl. He stared malevolently at Traynor. "You have brought me nothing but a girl of the streets!"

"She is young, and pretty…." Traynor excused himself.

"I want innocent girls!" the evil Asiatic whispered. "I want none such as this! Go now, and see that you do better on your next four trips! Else your golden-haired wife will surely die, and you will lose her forever!"

"Oh, God…!" Traynor breathed frantically. And he turned, swayed blindly out into the night once more.

And this time he resolutely avoided those few *nymphs du pave* who might have accosted him as he wandered through the rain. Wu Chang wanted no more of that sort….! He wanted more innocent blood…!

At last Traynor came to a looming apartment building. Guided only by instinct and a dull, dazed intuition, he found the fire-escape that led upward. Almost without volition he climbed the wet, rusty, latticed steps; until suddenly he stopped upon a certain landing, saw a light gleaming from a window.

He peered in; perceived a tiled bathroom. Out from under a shower a young girl stepped. A young girl, and beautiful; a girl with boyish breasts and graceful hips and columnar thighs of creamy smoothness. She began toweling herself—

Dent Traynor smashed through the glass of the window. The girl screamed—once. Then he was upon her. His hand fell across her mouth, stifling her cries. He crushed her savagely, held her, pinioned her. He could feel her firm little breasts against his chest as she squirmed and tried to fight free.

But he held her; and he managed somehow to uncork the vial of poisonous, colorless fluid; apply the saturated handkerchief to her nostrils.

She succumbed; she went limp in his arms.

Like an evil ghoul, he lifted her through the smashed window of the bathroom, sped with her down the fire-escape. And this time, when he showed his burden to Wu Chang, the sinister Asiatic smiled his toothless, leering smile.

"You have done better this time, O Dent Traynor!" the old man cackled. And he ran esurient, gnarled fingers over the young girl's rounded curves. "She is exactly what I need. See that you bring me three more like her."

TRAYNOR shuddered at the unholy note in Wu Chang's tone. "What will you do with this girl?" he whispered.

The Chinese shrugged. "She will die, of course. The blood from her corpse will help to save your wife from death, Dent Traynor. Already that first girl you brought here is dead. The poison you pressed upon her nostrils has done its work. Would you care to witness what use I am making of her blood?"

Traynor recoiled from a nameless horror that filled him. He did not want to witness whatever fiendish necromancy the old man used; had no desire to see the demoniac, sinister magic which Wu Chang must employ in his dark sorceries. And yet… those dark sorceries would bring the lovely Lola back to radiant health....

"Yes!" he forced himself to say. "Let me see what you do with the blood of the girls I bring here."

"Then come." Wu Chang turned, led Traynor upstairs to the room where Lola lay white and pallid upon a bed, like a corpse which still faintly breathed.

The Chinese picked up a brass bowl carved with intricate, evil, hideous figures. The bowl was filled with a turgid, slime-like, ruby-red substance of gelatinous density; a sort of red, liquified jelly that quivered in the depths of the bowl....

"What stuff is that?" Traynor whispered; but he knew, even before he asked the question, what Wu Chang's answer would be.

"It is blood!" the sinister old man cackled. "Blood fresh from the corpse of the brunette street-girl you brought to me. Blood drawn from her warm veins after she had died from the poison you had pressed upon her nostrils. Blood—from the first girl you killed!"

"God...!" Dent mumbled thickly.

He watched as Wu Chang took the brass bowl to a far corner of the room; watched as the Asiatic placed the bowl upon a charcoal brazier. And as the heat stirred nauseous bubbles in the blood-filled bowl, Wu Chang dropped a pinch of grey, sparkling powder in the hell's broth.

The brew simmered; and from its red surface arose a dense cloud of stenchlike vapor—a charnel-house odor, sickening and foul, like the stink of rotting corpses and putrescent human flesh....

Then Wu Chang removed the brass bowl, stirred the warm blood until it had cooled sufficiently for him to place his evil fingers into the mixture. Cackling, he went to Lola where she lay unconscious upon the bed. He drew back the covers, baring her to the waist. And Traynor saw that his lovely bride was nude; that her sleeping-garment had been removed from her white, nubile body. Again to Dent came a wave of throttled rage, that the evil Wu Chang should look upon Lola's nudity with his glittering and desirous eyes.

NOW Wu Chang was muttering weird incantations in some lost, eerie tongue and he dipped his fingers in the blood within the hideous brass bowl. He smeared the viscid, crimson stuff upon Lola's lovely breasts; and either in reality or imagination, Dent thought that the old man's hands lingered over-long upon that delicious cream-white feminine flesh as the sickening red slime was spread....

Then, even as he watched, Traynor's pulses commenced to hammer savagely. Lola had stirred upon the bed! At the touch of Wu Chang's blood-stained hand and the sound of his hellish incantations, she moved a little!

Wu Chang turned. "You see, Traynor!" he triumphed. "My magic will do its work! Already your wife moves. With the blood of four more young girls, she will be completely cured!"

"You mean—?"

"Go out again, O Dent Traynor! Go out and bring me more victims, that I may finish my black sorcery!"

Like a man bereft of reason, insane with sudden hope, Traynor turned and raced from the room, from the house. His lovely Lola would live again! She would laugh, and sing, and dance! And he would hold her in his arms, as he had always done; he would hold her, and caress her, and kiss her upon the lips! He would know the sweetness of her, the warmth of her fragrant, taut breasts; he would know the heat of her love....

And what if this all be at the cost of five murders? What did it matter if Dent stained his soul with the blood of five innocent victims? So great was his love for his yellow-haired bride that he no longer thought of his lost, lost soul. His hands would be stained with innocent blood; there would be five murders upon his conscience and his heart; but his lovely Lola would live again!

Grimly he stifled his horror at what he had already done; and at what he still must do. Two girls he had already slain; three more must he murder with Wu Chang's evil poison.... But he fought down the revulsion that ate at his vitals. It was almost as if he were two men; one standing aside helplessly, revolted by the evil which the other wrought.

Evil! Dent Traynor knew, now, that he had become a thing of

evil—like the slant-eyed, sinister Wu Chang himself. He had become a murderer, and he would murder again—three times again. He had sold his everlasting soul to the devil; but he no longer cared. Under the hypnosis of hope that Wu Chang could cure the beautiful, yellow-haired Lola, Traynor's better nature lost its unequal battle with evil. And he no longer cared….

Grimly he departed from Wu Chang's ominous, demon-reeking house. Grimly he started forth in the rain to seek a new feminine victim—

What was that?

AGAIN he heard it—a wailing, mournful, tortured scream in the rain-drenched night. The scream of someone in uttermost terror-depths; the scream of a woman subjected to nameless fears!

And the sound came from within Wu Chang's ominous house!

It was the scream of Traynor's lovely, golden-haired wife! *The scream of Lola Traynor!*

A sudden curse, half prayer and half blasphemy, leaped to Traynor's lips. He turned, smashed himself at the front door through which he had just come. *It was locked from within!*

He backed off, gathered his tense muscles, bashed his body at the portal. This time his hurtling, plummeted weight catapulted upon the door with pile-driver force; with the berserk force of a human batter-ram. The wood splintered. The door swung inward on twisted hinges.

Like a madman, Dent went leaping for the stairs. At the foot of the steps there was a pot-bellied, evil Oriental idol of bronze; and as Traynor neared it, *the thing moved!*

It split apart; revealed itself as a hollow shell. And from within that shell, a slant-eyed and leering Chinese hatchetman leaped— straight for Traynor's throat.

Traynor side-stepped. His foot caught in a small throw-rug; he went off-balance. The leering hatchetman was upon him now. Dent Traylor felt a bashing concussion upon his skull as his assailant bludgeoned him with an upraised blackjack. Again there came a smashing, brain-jarring blow. Dent Traynor went down in a dazed, semi-stupefied sprawl.

He felt the hatchetman jabbing something into his ribs; saw that the object was a snug-snouted automatic. "Arise!" the Chinese cutthroat hissed. "Arise, that I may take you to my master, Wu Chang. He will deal with you for smashing his front door."

Staggering, swaying on his feet, Traynor was prodded up the stairway, along the hallway of the upper floor. His captor stopped him before a closed door. It was the door of the room where Dent's lovely wife lay at the mercy of Wu Chang. And from within the room there sounded again a shrill scream of terror—

Lola's wailing, gibbering cry of insane and crystalline fear!

Then, as the ululant wail died down, there came another voice. It was the voice of the Chinese girl, Cherry-Blossom; she who was Lola's maid; she who had first suggested to Dent that he come here to seek Wu Chang's assistance.

CHERRY-BLOSSOM was speaking. "Listen, O my venerable father. You will be wise not to meddle with this yellow-haired woman, Lola Traynor. Be content with the five girls whom Dent Traynor will bring to you. Leave this woman alone. Give her back to her husband when he has fulfilled his part of the bargain and brought you five girls."

"Be still, my daughter!" came Wu Chang's evil snarl.

"But my father, you do not need this yellow-haired woman. I have a feeling that if you harm her, there will be disaster for you—"

"Attend me, daughter!" Wu Chang's voice rasped through the closed door of the room and impinged upon Traynor's listening ears. "Your task is to obtain positions with white families; to act as a maid; to feed my subtle coma-poison to each mistress for whom you work, even as you fed it to this golden-haired girl. After that, your work is done. After that, you have only to suggest my name as a possible doctor for the ill woman. The rest of the task belongs to me."

"I know that, my father. But—"

"There are no buts. You attend to your work, I attend to mine. When I have a victimized husband in my power, I force him to bring me five girls. He is duped into believing he has slain those five girls—he is fooled by the gelatin in the bowl, which I tell

Wu Chang snarled. "She is nothing but a girl of the streets!"

him is blood. He never realized that he has only chloroformed the five victims he has brought me; and that they will recover consciousness later—when I have placed them aboard a boat bound for the South American brothels. This flesh-traffic of ours is lucrative, my daughter; but I will brook none of your interference!"

"But listen, my father. It was not planned that you should also make this yellow-haired woman one of your slaves! Then why do you now seek to have her—?"

Outside the door, returning consciousness brought a red tide of raging fury to Traynor's heart. So that was it! His lovely Lola had not been ill of some mysterious disease; she had been drugged! Drugged with some mysterious, potent sleeping-medicine! Drugged by the Chinese maid, Cherry-Blossom!

And the two girls whom Traynor had brought here—they had not died! He had not killed them with the liquid he had pressed upon their faces! He had only anaesthetized them—and brought them here so that the evil Wu Chang could sell them into white slavery!

And now Wu Chang planned that same fate for the lovely Lola!

HIS fury burst its bounds, sundered all restrain, erased all sanity and all caution; and Dent whirled upon the Chinese hatchetman who was his captor. He whirled—and struck at the man's gun-hand before the Asiatic could make a defensive move.

And then, while the automatic was deflected downward, Dent balled his fists and struck.

His knuckles bashed sickenly upon the hatchetman's jaw. The Chinese went down in sprawling unconsciousness. Dent snatched up the fallen man's gun; hurled himself at the closed door of the room before him.

There came a crashing sound of rending wood. Traynor leaped into the chamber; saw the evil Wu Chang holding Lola in his rapacious arms, stroking her white skin, breathing upon her face. And Lola was conscious—was fighting at the wizened, sinister yellow man, while Cherry-Blossom stood helplessly by.

"You foul fiend—!" Traynor roared. And he raised the automatic, squeezed the trigger.

But even as he fired, a strange thing happened. The Chinese girl, Cherry-Blossom, sprang into the line of fire. Loyal to the last, loyal to her heritage, loyal to her blood, she took the first bullet intended for her evil father. Took the slug in her heart, and went slumping down to death.

Wu Chang scuttled across the room, trying to escape. But there was no escape from the avenging rage that seethed in Traynor's heart. He fired again and again; sent a stream of scalding lead into Wu Chang's back. And even after the sinister old Asiatic was dead upon the floor, Traynor kept firing into the body, so that it bounced and jigged a macabre rigadoon upon the blood-stained rug....

And then Traynor had his lovely, unclad wife in his arms; felt her nearness and the warmth of her trembling body pressed close to his own. And he heard her sweet voice saying: "Dent—my darling—my sweet—you saved me from…!"

He held her, soothed her. "Come, my little bride. We will release the two girls I brought here tonight. And then—"

She needed no other words from him.

FALSE FACE

*This beautiful woman had the strange power
of compelling him to kill… even to murder
his own best friend. What would happen
when he woke up a different man…?*

Mc*CARTY crouched behind* the curtain and trembled like a man with ague. The perspiration that coated his forehead, trickled down onto his cheeks and chin, was icy cold. His eyes protruded, his tongue flicked nervously at taut lips. He gripped the slender handle of the wicked knife so hard that his nails made deep crescents in the palm of his hand.

Within the room Coleman, the tall, thin man, raised his drink shakily from the tabouret, his eyes on the woman in green. Loose lips tasted the spiced wine. Drops of purple drooled down his chin, fell on his white shirt bosom unheeded. Thickly he said, "God, you're beautiful!"

The woman smiled inscrutably from her seat of cushions. Her eyes were green, as green as the sheathlike dress she wore. The upper slopes of magnificent breasts were milk white in vivid contrast. The only other splotch of color about her was the deep crimson gash of her rouged lips closed over a long cigarette holder.

When she arose, all movement was liquid, like flowing water, rippling from those upthrust breasts to flaring, lyre-like hips, down through tapering thighs and aristocratic ankles.

Behind the velvet curtain McCarty moaned aloud, licked at the spittle that flecked his dry lips.

The skirt of the emerald gown was slit on the right side. White flesh was alabaster as the tall woman moved toward the man in the armchair. Carved ivory in a bed of jade.

Coleman gaped drunkenly. She sat on the arm of the chair and the perfume of her body was more heady than the wine. It was her slender fingers that held the wineglass to his mouth, her slender arm that pulled his tousled head close to her bosom.

Coleman's hot lips left a scar of purple wine on the whiteness of her throat. She held him close, her eyes alight with strange fires. Coleman's arms were about her, his hands eager, caressing.

ACROSS his shoulder she looked at the velvet curtains that sheltered McCarty. It was as if those slotted green eyes had the power to draw the hangings aside to reveal the man who crouched there, knife in hand.

Her crimson lips made an audible sound, "Now!" Coleman's eyes were closed, his mouth pressed to the fragrant softness of her throat.

Slowly, like a man in a trance, McCarty parted the curtains and stepped into the room. He did not look at Coleman. He did not look to right or left; his gaze was unflinchingly on the green eyes of the woman. He was, perhaps, ten feet from her. In traversing those ten feet he thought of many things like a man who faces execution and reviews his entire life in the brief instant before the trap is sprung.

This man Coleman was his friend, had been his friend since boyhood. This man Coleman was a dupe, an innocent pawn in a game. It had been McCarty himself who brought him to the woman, who brought him to his doom.

"I can't do it, I can't do it," something sang in his brain. But the inexorable eyes of the emerald lady drew him on. Her lips were smiling triumphantly now. She knew she had won, knew McCarty would do her bidding.

She pressed Coleman closer to her heaving breasts. Her hand stroked his neck, up and down, her fingers stealing through his hair like white serpents. For a moment McCarty poised behind the chair, almost forgetful of the gleaming knife in his hand. Green eyes held his. Slender fingers gently pulled the collar away from a thin brown throat. Red lips softly said, "Here!"

McCarty, fascinated, thrust the death weapon deep into the throat of his best friend.

The woman's arms tightened as the victim's body tensed con-

vulsively. His death scream was silenced by the pressure of her breasts. The only audible sounds were the sighing of McCarty, the murderer, and the laughter of the green woman. But Coleman, with a last convulsive effort leaped erect, dragging the woman with him. She fell to the floor, pinned by the twitching corpse. The grey rug beneath them turned crimson, the woman lay supine, eyes afire, red mouth laughing, laughing.

A heavy set little man came through the door. His face was lemon colored, his eyes back behind the thick lenses of pince nez glasses that were attached to his thick bosom by a black ribbon. He rubbed hairy hands together, chuckled in his thick throat. Slowly he rolled the corpse from the woman.

For a moment she lay there, still laughing. McCarty shuddered. The emerald dress was clotted with blood, gouts of blood, wrig-

She hurled the bottle; it crashed behind him.

gling snakes of blood. The white flesh above the dress was crimson. The long tapering leg of ivory that emerged from the slit skirt was flecked with crimson, tiny red poppies on a field of snow. Poppies of death.

Slowly she got to her feet. Methodically the thick one, who looked like a fat spider, went about his work. He took everything from the pockets of the dead man. He cut laundry marks and labels from his clothes. He pulled him to the center of the room, folded the once gray carpet over him. He looked at the woman.

"Your dress," he said.

She shrugged her way from it, tossed it in the dead man's face. A scanty triangle of emerald chiffon clung to full hips. Emerald slippers on slim feet, emerald chiffon about full hips, emerald eyes above a cruel red mouth. Crimson, crimson—the slash of her lips. Crimson, crimson the streaks of blood that crisscrossed unfettered breasts.

Green eyes summoning white faced McCarty. Red lips murmuring, "Lover, lover, you did it, you did it for me!" Ivory arms about McCarty's neck. An ivory body pressing closely to him, alabaster breasts flattening against his shirt bosom. Loose lips parting to receive his kiss, loose lips warm and moist. When she pulled away he wiped shakily at his mouth with the back of his hand. The back of his hand was crimson with lipstick. Or blood.

THE moonlight was silver on the quiet lake. The little cabin boat chuckled its way across the magic waters. A radio played softly in the cabin. McCarty lay on a padded locker, his eyes closed. Beside him sat the woman with the green eyes. Her fingers smoothed his hair, her cool palms stroked his fevered cheeks. On deck at the wheel, the thick-set Portuguese, De Sylva, the fat spider who had taken the corpse. Presently he called softly, "Sara, Sara. This is the place."

McCarty opened tortured eyes at the sound of her voice. The woman leaned to kiss him, poured a stiff drink into a water glass. She said softly, caressingly, "Stay here, darling. You've done your part." Then she was gone.

On deck a shapeless gray bundle lay in the shadow of the cabin. Close examination would have proved it to be a grey rug wrapped tightly and sewn about a corpse. The end of the corpse was inserted into a tub of muddy appearing stuff.

Sara Dunkirk, the green eyed woman said, "Has the cement set?" Her voice was as hard as the cement. De Sylva, the Portuguese nodded, came from the wheel to help her push the weighted bundle from the thirty foot cruiser. It made hardly a splash. Only a growing ripple in the silver water showed where the murdered man had disappeared.

THE same moon shone through the open window at McCarty's home to gild a silver square on a bed. In the middle of the picture, Ruth McCarty, the murderer's wife. She slept fit-

She pulled his head down suddenly, pointed to the spot for the knife.

fully, golden hair haloing the oval of her face, one white arm flung high on the pillow. The gauzy nightdress fell away to reveal the fullness of deeply breathing breasts, satin white, and alluring. A sound awakened her. For a moment she lay wide-eyed in the moonlight, her face twisted with fear.

She turned, saw that the space beside her was empty. She turned on a table lamp. Twelve twenty. Something kept roaring in her brain like an approaching storm that threatens to sweep everything before it. The echo of her troubled dream appeared and reappeared. "Robert," she murmured to herself, "something has happened to Robert!" The feeling was so strong that she could hardly force herself to lie back down. Grimly she switched off the light, grimly she closed her eyes. Robert had been staying out more and more of late; there was nothing to worry about. She half slept, half dozed.

Again the light. Two thirty, exactly. A key in the door. Hurriedly she turned out the light. She heard his staggering footsteps as he entered, somehow realized that they were not so much the footsteps of a drunken man as those of an old man, querulous, uncertain, half reeling.

She knew he was in the room, smelled the liquor. She heard his clothes flung to the floor, the thump of his empty shoes. Again those padding footsteps as he went to the bathroom. The sound of running water. Minutes past.

He had left the door open. Puzzled she sat up in the bed, thrust out a rounded leg. From the door she peered toward the bathroom. He was at the lavatory scrubbing his hands, head bent low. The soap was thick on his fingers, his palms, his wrists. He was muttering like a man in a daze. He washed the soap off, peered at his white hands and still muttering lathered them again. Raising, his image appeared in the mirror.

Ruth McCarty clutched her breasts in fear. The face in the mirror was haggard, deeply lined, the eyes half mad. "Robert," involuntarily. He did not hear her. He went on slowly, savagely scrubbing his hands.

EVEN the bank officials where McCarty worked tried to keep it out of the papers but the prying news-hounds were too much for them. Headlines screamed:

> "First National Looted of $220,000 in Cash and Negotiable Securities by Absconding Teller. Samuel G. Coleman Sought Throughout States and Foreign Countries."

Both Mrs. McCarty and the bank officials attributed McCarty's sudden nervous collapse to the fact that Coleman was his best friend, that duty alone had made him report the loss and theft himself. The officials gave him a two weeks' leave of absence to recover from the shock. Ruth treated him as if nothing had come between them. Gradually he grew back to normalcy, but he never ceased that awful scrubbing, scrubbing of his hands from time to time….

The postman brought the package. It was a small square block, possibly two inches in each dimension. There was no name; it was merely addressed to the house number. Ruth opened it. That evening she spoke to Robert McCarty about it, showed it to him. His face blanched, his eyes burned, lines appeared again about his mouth.

The package held a solitary carnation. The carnation had been dyed emerald green.

SARA met him at the door, her seductive body clothed in the inevitable color. He did not take off his hat, but thrust her aside and walked into the living room. "Call De Sylva," he said. She smiled, called the Portuguese.

Back and forth paced McCarty trying not to look at Sara Dunkirk's crossed legs, at the ivory skin of round thighs flowing into secretive skirt shadows above dark, sheer stockings; trying not to see the shadowed valley between her breasts when she leaned forward for a cigarette. De Sylva sat in the corner and said nothing. His eyes were expressionless behind the thick lenses of his glasses.

McCarty said, "I come to tell you I'm through, Sara. I've tried to think, tried to reason it out. There's nothing else for me to do. You hold some sort of power over me, you can make me do your will. You forced me to kill my best friend, you forced me to steal from the bank and lay the blame on him. We are all equally guilty so there is nothing you can do to prevent my quitting. I awake in the night to see Coleman's face peering at me. I can't stand it any longer. My wife looks at me as if she knew what I had done. Rather than risk that again, I'm quitting."

The woman smiled, her lips twisted, "You don't love me any more? Look at me!"

Instead he looked away, fumbled at the tabouret for a drink. De Sylva rumbled in his throat, "Don't be a fool. We've pulled the perfect crime. Tonight we bring it to its conclusion. Manning comes to buy the bonds!"

"I want no part of them!" He raved on. De Sylva caught Sara's eye, got up and left the room on silent feet. The woman walked across to the radio, her hips swaying seductively. For a moment she fumbled at the dials. The strains of a waltz filled the room.

"And this is goodbye?"

"Yes," desperately.

"Dance with me, then."

Her eyes were green flames. Slowly he walked toward her, unable to resist. They danced. The slim waist beneath the palm of his right hand was like fire. He felt muscles ripple beneath velvet skin, felt soft flesh give to his hot fingers. Her arm was frankly about his neck, her red mouth close to his cheek. He tried to keep from looking at her, tried to keep his eyes on the ivory rise and fall of her breasts.

As if drawn by a magnet he raised his head, looked into those long green slots. His arm tightened savagely, he groaned. Her body pressed his, her back arched. Still moaning he leaned to press a savage kiss on her loose lips and in the back of his mind he knew she was twisting him about her slim finger once again.

MANNING, the fence, was short and fat, jovial appearing like a good natured padre. Only his thick lips wet and shiny showed his sensual side. His little deepset eyes twinkled as if with good humor alone as he counted the money out on the table. He said, "I'd like to give you more, Sara, but you know I may have to hold the bonds a few years."

She laughed, tucked the money into a drawer. "Let's have a drink on it, Manning. I'm satisfied."

He followed her across the room, his eyes glowing at sight of the lithe body beneath the thin dress. Minutes passed.

Behind the curtain McCarty watched with wide eyes. This time there was no horror in his mind, only a strange exultation. His eyes glowed, he licked at wet lips, he raised the thin knife and smiled at it, tested its sharpness with his fingertip. His eyes were fixed on the spot above Manning's collar where he hoped to drive the knife point.

LATER it was McCarty who held the ivory woman in his arms and laughed down at the bloody lifeless thing that had once been a man.

Green eyes gazed curiously at the laughing man. He swept her into his arms, gazed deep into green eyes that still held and fascinated. "I don't hate you," he exulted, "I love you. Whatever I am, you've made me!"

A few weeks later Robert McCarty quit his job at the bank. Ruth, his wife, watched his growing strangeness apprehensively. She tried to win him back to her with seductive clothing, by revealing her charms indiscriminately. But gradually she grew more and more frightened of the strange look in his eyes. They seemed to be changing color.

He discarded a safety razor for a keen edged straight blade and took pleasure in shaving himself twice a day. Often Ruth peered in the bathroom to find him scraping at his throat with the sharp blade, his lips twisted in a grimace, his eyes gloating and mad as the steel glided across his flesh.

Toby, the white Persian with the green eyes brushed against his legs one morning as he shaved. He looked down. The cat *miaowed*, its green eyes peered up at him. Quick as a flash McCarty snatched it from the floor. The razor made a slashing arc in the air. The cat screamed once then thudded to the bathtub the blood streaming from its white throat.

It was minutes before McCarty could quit laughing. Afterward he wrapped the body in a bath towel, wrapped brown paper about it and carried it away from the house. Still the insatiable bloodlust was on him. He went to the woman Sara.

De Sylva came in that night to find them entwined in each other's arms on the divan. As always Sara wore green to match her eyes. Her exposed flesh was milk-white in contrast. De Sylva said, "You drunken fools, you're going to get us caught yet. McCarty quits his job and spends all his time with you!"

But neither paid any attention. They were lost in each other. She leaned to press her lips against the throbbing jugular in McCarty's throat. He thrilled at the sharp pain of her teeth, drew her closer. Her eyes were green flames.

LATER she whispered, "De Sylva is too bossy. If he were out of the way the money and bonds would be ours alone."

McCarty sat up and grinned shyly. Near midnight the fat body of De Sylva went over the side of the pleasure yacht.

Again the moon in the window when McCarty reached home, a natural spotlight that illuminated the curved body of his wife. Undressing, he lay down beside her, raised up on one elbow and peered down at her. The whiteness of her breasts, the steady breathing of her torso! He saw the tiny *throb throb throb* of the pulse at her temple, allowed his gloating eyes to seek and find the pulse at the base of her throat.

When she awakened the next morning she found the razor on the pillow beside her head. Robert McCarty was gone. Something must have snapped in his brain, for he suddenly realized that he had become a thirster after blood. To his warped mind there was but one thing to do—to put miles between his wife and himself, for he knew that the only way he wanted to possess her now was through death. He had taken no clothing, but with a mad man's inconsistency had thrust a small picture of Charles Coleman into his coat pocket.

As the plane roared on into the west he closed his eyes to shut out the vision of the throbbing pulse at the base of her throat. Even then the appearing vision was hateful for it changed swiftly to a pair of slotted green eyes.

ROBERT McCARTY was one of the three survivors dug out of the wreckage of the huge transport plane. Unconscious for weeks, they despaired time and again of his life, but he pulled through. He had taken the trip under an assumed name and there was no one to notify.

He returned to consciousness to find a white clad nurse leaning over him. "Where am I? Who am I?" he faltered. The nurse called an interne, who labored long moments with him trying to convince him his name was Smith, that he had been in an airplane accident, that they had rebuilt his features. But there was no responsive spark in McCarty's battered mind. He could not recall an iota of the past. His murders, the woman Sara, his wife, all were as if they had never existed.

Some seventh sense warned him however that all was not as it should be, so he kept silent. Several thousand dollars in cash and large bills had been in his pockets. He was discharged from the hospital months later, rather well to do. Yet he couldn't recall where he had obtained the money. Often he took a battered picture from his pocket and peered at it. *This was the photo he had been carrying in the crash, the photo the doctors had used as a model in remodeling his crushed features.*

McCarty made money. In the course of the months that followed he engaged in business enterprises that were more than fortunate. A year passed. His business expanded, he went east to meet some of his customers.

There was something vaguely familiar about the town, something that stirred a responsive chord in the back of his being. Business concluded, he set out in search of pleasure and was deposited at the "Jade Lantern" by a taxi driver.

Seated alone at a table he watched the semi-nude dancers of the chorus without interest. The club itself held him. He felt convinced that he had been there before, not once but many times, not alone but with someone.

Henri, the headwaiter, approached to see if the service had been all right. Ever since McCarty entered Henri had watched, puzzled wonder in his eyes. Now, bowing obsequiously he gazed directly at McCarty. Leaving the table he went directly to a phone booth.

Almost at the same moment McCarty felt a burning gaze directed at him, turned to stare into a pair of green eyes, to smile at a red mouth which was itself parted in challenge.

Sara Dunkirk was alone. Above the white tablecloth only a little of an emerald evening gown was visible. The svelte breasts beneath it, half exposed, were as white as the tablecloth! Her smile was a summons and McCarty obeyed.

RED—FOR MURDER

*John Hunter knew women! At least, he thought
he did. It took a flood and a girl who wouldn't
let her heart overcome her head to show him
that no man can really understand women!*

J OHN HUNTER *knew* women, knew how to play
on their emotions, their sympathies and vanities, as a master
artist plays on a violin. Women were his profession. He knew that
his very slightness, his boyish face, his impulsive actions, all awakened the mothering instinct of the average woman. And John
Hunter loved it!

Now, as he sat dejectedly on a divan, head in hands, he peered
between the fingers that covered his eyes and watched Frieda
James pace the floor, tears coming from her brown eyes, hands
clenched into fists as she talked.

Frieda James was tall, nearly as tall as Hunter. Her breasts were
high and firm, her body willowy and lithe, from slightly flaring
hips to tapering thighs and finely chiseled ankles. Her hair was
auburn, a deep auburn, and her skin that milk white allurement
of all red headed women.

Hunter peered cautiously at her as she paced the floor, watched
with appreciation the quiver of soft hips beneath thin material,
the gentle sway of half-fettered breasts. Appreciation, yes, but in
his heart he was damning her, cursing her for coming to her senses
just as well laid plans were about to mature. He managed a deep
sigh as she paused before him, looked at his dejected figure with
pity in her eyes. John Hunter could act, when business required
it.

"Don't be so hurt, darling," she said, and touched his hair with
long fingers. "Don't you see that I just couldn't do it? I thought I
could go through with it. I even got the stuff from my husband's

safe, brought it here with me tonight, ready to leave with you. Then I thought of the family, thought of poor dad, what the disgrace would mean to him. No, John, it isn't right. We must think of the others."

She fell to her knees before him, put her head in his lap, and cried brokenly. His fingers strayed to her hair, stroked the whiteness of her neck, the smooth softness of trembling shoulders. He leaned to bury his mouth and face in the auburn hair, muttering, "It's all right, dear, I understand. But it's hard—hard—"

Even as his hands caressed her, as his lips kissed her, his eyes were narrowed, shrewd. In himself he was cursing her for a fool. To himself he said, *"But she opened the safe and got the stuff. She brought it here with her."* And he knew then, with a little thrill of terror, what he was going to do.

THEY had met, several months before, at a cocktail party. Hunter, ever on the alert, knew at once who she was. Wife of Bernard James, wealthy broker and man about town. Daughter of Sheldon Morgan, financier, and head of one of the town's oldest and proudest families. There were three Morgan children, two girls, Frieda and Anna, and a brother, George. All had been known for their wildness in their more youthful days, and old Sheldon Morgan had spent a great deal of money keeping their antics off the front pages. All this John Hunter knew when he first met Frieda.

It took him another week to find that Frieda was unhappily married, that the wild strain still persisted in her blood in spite of maturity. After that, it had been easy. Before the month was over, they were close friends. Another month and they were lovers, meeting surreptitiously in the little apartment Hunter rented for their stolen rendezvous.

NOW, as he caressed her thinly clad body, he thought bitterly that those past months had been wasted. Just as he had gotten her to the point of leaving her husband, sense of family honor intervened. So near and yet so far!

She had even taken cash and securities from her husband's safe and brought them with her as he had planned! And at the last

His fingers closed remorselessly. Then he had the money.

moment, here she was backing out. His original plan had been actually to take her away with him, for a few weeks at least, then to get rid of her as quietly as possible. He knew Sheldon Morgan would restore the money to Bernard James, the husband, to keep the scandal quiet. And he knew he was utterly safe, for the same reason. And now she was throwing him.

Slowly he unwound her arms, got to his feet. Yes, John Hunter was an actor. His voice was filled with infinite pain, his eyes were those of a hurt dog. Slowly he walked away from her, poured a drink at the table and tossed it off before turning to her.

"It's all right, Frieda. I might have known it was only a game to you. But it's all right."

"How can you say that?" She was before him now, breasts heaving tumultuously, lithe body straining toward him. "Haven't

I given you everything? Haven't we meant everything to each other? I'll always be yours!"

"You'll always be mine!" His voice was husky.

His hand shot out to hook curved fingers in the vee of her negligee. The garment gave with a tiny tearing sound, dropped to her waist. Proud and unashamed she stood before him, her skin gleaming like satin, her bosom, blue veined mounds of pal-

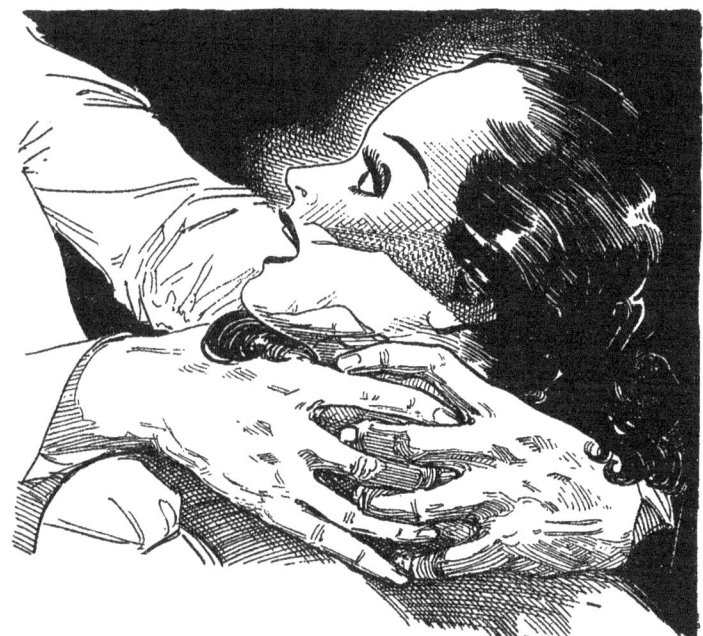

pitant flesh under a lacy brassiere, her torso and hips like finely carved marble by a master sculptor.

"It's goodbye, darling," he muttered, and swept her to him. A sob escaped her as his hand wound into the auburn mass of her hair, as her breasts flattened against his chest and her body swayed close against his. His lips were on the tiny hollow at the base of her throat as he picked her up in his arms....

LONG afterward she was still in the circle of his arms with closed eyes and parted lips. Gently, gently his fingers caressed the soft column of her throat. Deep inside of him a voice was saying exultantly, *"Now! Now! You fool!"* His fingers tightened slightly. She stirred, half moaned, opened her eyes. And then she understood.

She knew the brooding, black dagger-points peering into her own eyes were the eyes of Death. She knew the red, raw slit of his mouth was a promise of death, that the ten sinewy fingers about her white throat were Death's executioners, merciless and relentless.

She struggled, flailed with white legs, clawed at him with frantic fingers, beat at him with futile fists. He merely ducked his head, shielded it by the soft cushion of her breast and held his relentless grip. Slowly her struggles subsided, slowly her quivering body quit thrashing. He relaxed his grip as if unwillingly, as if his fingers had enjoyed the act. Something dribbled down into his eyes. He wiped it away, saw that it was blood, where she had scratched him.

Like a drunken man he glared at her, muttered thickly, "Damn you!" His left hand wound itself into her hair, half raised her from the pillow. His right, clenched into a bony fist, drove against her jaw. She catapulted back onto the pillow, sprawled still and limp and silent, red, red blood slowly trickling from her mouth, down onto her throat, seeping in little irregular rivulets down across her two flawless breasts. Curiously he looked at his left hand. It was filled with red hair, hair that had been torn from her head when he drove her backward onto the pillow. With a grimace of repulsion he tossed it at the still figure and glared about the room.

THERE was her overnight bag, on the vanity stool! He opened it, eyes glowing. Three thick sacks of greenbacks, four packets of bonds. He leafed through them exultantly, transferred them to a black briefcase, and went to the bathroom to wash up. Carefully he daubed the dried blood from the scratch on his face, scrubbed his hands meticulously. He felt safe, utterly safe. For he knew that Frieda James had told no one of this apartment, knew that it might be days before her body was discovered, and that he would be miles away before that time. To hell with the Morgans and the James! Let them try to catch him!

He entered the automatic elevator, briefcase beneath his arm. As he pressed the proper button with his left thumb, the light flickered and gleamed on the ring on his middle finger. It was a double cameo, deeply, sharply cut. He peered at it more closely, laughed a little, grimly. For twined in the ring, beneath the band and about the sharp cut stone, were half a dozen long red hairs.

Suddenly he was nauseated as the realization of his murder swept over him. White-faced, he remembered the still, warm body upstairs on the bed, the body that he had known so well. Horror smote him. He tore the ring and its intertwined hairs from his hand, and was twisting it in his fingers as the elevator car came to a stop. The door slid open, and the ring dropped to the floor. He stooped, but it eluded him, slid between the car and the ground-floor landing of the building. On hurrying feet he went through the deserted lobby, through the swing-door onto the wet street. He couldn't wait to look for the ring. Undoubtedly it had dropped to the basement and he would have to let it go.

Rain pattered about him as he hailed a cab. Rain pattered rhythmically on the roof of the cab as they rolled away, pattered like tiny accusing fingers. Once he turned on the cab light and looked wonderingly at his own hands. Somehow they were still warm, as if from the touch of Frieda's flesh. He closed his eyes quickly, stopped the cab at a bar and sat in a booth for the next half hour getting a grip on himself. Even inside, it seemed he could hear the steady swish-swish of the beating storm.

LATER, when liquor had calmed the tumult within him, he stood in a garage on the opposite side of town while a greasy attendant brought his car. "Bad night for driving, Mr. Smith," said the man, getting from behind the wheel. Hunter merely nodded. He had stored the car here three days before under the name of Smith. Now he gave the man a bill, got in, rolled slowly out on the rainswept street. The windshield wipers clicked methodically, the rain beat against the glass, drummed against the top.

Damn it all, he couldn't go it alone. John Hunter was used to companionship, had to have it. The thought of a long trip to be made by himself, with the remembrance of the still white body of Frieda James to haunt him, was more than he could stand. So he headed the dark car toward the *Silver Slipper.*

HE was waiting on a littered divan in her dressing room when she came in after her first number. Changes were made quickly at the *Silver Slipper* and the scanty net brassiere was swinging in her hand as she came through the door. Her breasts, powdered white, were full and generous. The scanty silk that cradled lush, full hips, was skin tight. He had her in his arms before she was aware of his presence. Finally she drew away from him, laughing.

He threw the car keys after the money. "Get out before I kill you!" he said.

"Johnny the Lush, drunk again! Let me go, honey, I'll see you after a while."

His voice was a little thick as he answered, "I'll never let you go, Belle. We're going away together, you and I. We're in the bucks, babe!"

Her eyes narrowed a little, calculatingly. "Interesting, if true." They sat down, close together, the soft flesh of her hip warm against his leg. He pulled a well-stuffed wallet from his pocket, She glimpsed the thick sheaf of bills within. He withdrew one, tossed it into her lap. "Five hundred on account," he said, "on account of the trip we're going to take."

Silence for a moment. Then, "I'm sick of this joint, Johnny. I'll go with you, as long as the jack holds out!" She opened her arms, slid them about his neck. Her body was warm and soft against him, he breathed deeply as he cradled her in his own caressing arms. Then his mouth was on her parted lips, her arms were pulling him down… down… down….

LONG moments later he pulled erect, stared at her curiously with haggard eyes. *His fingers hurt.* It was as if they were cramped, as if he could not straighten them. Fascinated, he stared at her white throat, where the tiny pulse-beat flickered rhythmically. She struggled erect, half fearful of something she read in his eyes, drew herself away from him, shivering. "What—?" she began, and stopped.

Now he was looking at her hair. The light poured down on it, lit it with a thousand copperish lights. "What the hell did you do to your hair?" he gasped.

"Nothing. Why? I had a little touch of henna put on it, but—"

She didn't understand his laughter, didn't understand why he snapped, "You can have it bleached tomorrow!"

THEY drove all that night with the storm unabated, with water pouring across the fingers of their headlights like a stream from a faucet. He was morose and silent, drinking steadily. After a while she dozed uncomfortably on the seat beside him. Once, stopping for a drink, he gazed at her through bloodshot eyes. Her coat had fallen apart, the low neck of her dress showed the upper slopes of her generous bosom, rising and falling steadily. The column of her throat—still powdered—the tiny pulse racing, racing at the soft base. *And again that ache in his fingers.*

"Great God," he thought, "am I going to strangle her? Why did I bring her?" But he decided the ache in his fingers was only a cramp from so much driving.

She awakened to find the car parked before a postoffice in a small town. The rain was still pouring; Hunter was gone. Through the steamy side window she saw him emerge from the postoffice, duck his head against the rain, and make for the car.

"No time to eat now," he said grimly. "The hick in there told me the levee may go any minute. We're going to Carsonville, babe, before the road is washed out. Damn the rain!"

THEY made Carsonville by noon, registered at the new hotel as Mr. and Mrs. John Berger. Instead of eating, he went directly to the bar.

Two hours later he went upstairs to find her asleep. She had unpacked for both of them, had laid his toilet array on the dresser. Nervously he threw off his coat, washed in the bathroom, and came back to the dresser. He picked up the comb, started. He cast it aside, horror and nausea sweeping him. Belle had used his comb. There were strands of woman's hair between its teeth, strands of hair that gleamed with a touch of red in the electric light.

And he thought again of the woman he had murdered. The whiskey he gulped from the half emptied bottle was like so much water. He walked across the room, stood staring at the sleeper. The gown had slid from her rounded white shoulders. Blue veined breasts were unbelievably alluring. For a moment a wave of warmth swept through his veins.

But as he sat beside her and kissed her moist lips, pulling her close to him, *he suddenly found that one of his hands was sliding beneath the nape of her neck to twine in her thick hair. Found that the other hand was caressing the base of her throat tentatively, thumb and forefinger contracting to squeeze the soft flesh.* She stirred restlessly, murmured, "Don't hurt me, honey," and reached to pull him close to the warmness and softness that was her pulsing body.

It was too much for Hunter. He knew now what he wanted to do. His urge toward this woman was unmistakable now. *He wanted to kill her.*

Her eyes opened, she read the madness in his own stare. Somehow she fought him off, though the gown was torn from her in the struggle.

"You damned drunk," she panted, "have you gone crazy?" There was a red bruise at the base of her throat, another splotch on a soft white shoulder where his fist had struck.

"You'll have to go," he said hoarsely. "Don't argue, just go, that's all. Here, damn it, get out before I kill you!" He tossed a handful of bills on the disheveled bed, threw the car keys after them. "Take the car, take anything, only get away before I kill you. I don't want to hang!" His voice arose to a shriek.

He cowered there against the bathroom door while she packed and dressed, left the room with never a goodbye. Something within her told her she had escaped death all too narrowly.

Later he wrapped his curved hands in hot towels, but couldn't relieve the painful ache that infested them.

ALL through the next forty-eight hours the sullen grey heaven poured down its burden. Most of that time Hunter spent at the bar, listening to the radio reports. Dykes burst, levees went out. Roaring rivers spread their turbulent waters over bottom lands, crawled higher and higher toward the bluffs and hills surrounding Carsonville. Hunter was glad.

In the isolation of the flood who would suspect John Berger of being John Hunter, the killer of Frieda James? The news bulletins made no mention of her death. "Either," he told himself, "they haven't found her yet or her old man, Sheldon Morgan, is paying money to keep it off the front pages again." He almost felt safe and smug about it. Until lonesomeness got him. John Hunter was a man who required companionship.

HE saw her first at the bar, of course, noticed her in the mirror. She was tall and slender, with great sullen brown eyes and a red mouth whose quirk spelled discontent. She crawled on a barstool with no regard for the expanse of chiffon leg her sliding dress disclosed. There was discontent apparent in every line of her body, every gesture she made.

When she returned his frank stare, she was insolent, even taunting, and when she walked from the barroom, knowing his eyes were following her, her full hips undulated provocatively beneath the silken material of her sheathlike dress.

Hunter grinned to himself, ordered another drink and went upstairs to change.

THEY dined together that night, for women were John Hunter's business. He knew how to ingratiate himself quickly and completely. She wore a daring gown of clinging velvet, backless, of extreme cut in the front. When she leaned across the table toward him, the deep, dusky valley of her alluring bosom was a tempting shadow. He found that she was Lita Strawn, married to a tobacco planter down the river. The bursting levees had endangered their house and her husband had sent her to Carsonville and safety. Later they drank together in the bar, stools pulled very close, while they listened to radio reports of the flooded valley.

Hunter scented fresh prey. He was always on the alert. He noted with satisfaction that she seemed to like him, that when her knee was against his own she made no effort to withdraw it, that often, when she moved, the warmth of a soft breast touched his elbow. So when he suggested cocktails in his own room, it was no surprise to find her assenting readily. The surprise really came when he found that her room adjoined his!

There was soft music on the room radio, mellow liquor on the tabouret. All men like talking of themselves and Lita Strawn encouraged John Hunter. Not that he told the truth, but he enjoyed building himself up in this woman's eyes. Later, he held her in his arms, kissed the insolent blotch of her crimson mouth and knew the avidity of practiced lips. Someway the shoulder straps of her gown slid down.

He knew the soft fullness of her breasts against his chest, saw the gleaming whiteness of curved thighs when her dress crawled higher and higher. She sighed, looked at him through half veiled eyes, with tremulous lips and a figure that trembled at his caress.

He laughed to himself when he reached for the light. After all, this was business to John Hunter....

MUCH later they took a farewell drink together. Hunter had already had too much and knew it. But the last drink somehow seemed to knock him out completely. His voice grew thick, maudlin, and his eyes began to glaze. He was conscious of the fact that she laughed at him, helped him with his coat and shoes and pushed him into the bed. Then thick sleep descended, black and deep, even blotting out the steady noise of the incessant rain.

THE next morning he stood before the dresser laughing like a madman. Her tap on the adjoining door brought him back to reality; he flung it wide. "What is it?" she gasped, appalled at the pallor of his face, the wildness of his eyes. "Have you been drinking already this morning?" She shook his shoulders but his laughter continued.

Slowly he extended his right hand. It held a comb, a man's comb. She took it curiously, humored him. "Naughty boy! There been a woman in your room and she used your comb!"

"But the hair," he managed, "it's red, oh God! It's red!" *Again there were strands of auburn hair caught in the teeth of the comb.*

She was with him all that day, sitting beside him while he babbled incoherently. She wrapped hot towels about his aching fingers, fingers that somehow could not seem to straighten out. And she gave him liquor constantly, whenever he asked for it.

That night she was still with him while he fought against the fear that raged within him. His hands seemed to feel soft flesh clutched within them. Again he saw the cameo ring with a few strands of red hair caught in the sharp stone. Hair from the head of the woman he had murdered. And again the comb, with the red hairs there to taunt him.

Outside the rain beat down, the flood crept higher and higher. There were boats patrolling the lower streets of Carsonville now. Telephone and telegraph lines went out earlier in the evening. Refugees clung to the precarious highlands about the town. Even the hotel lobby was crowded with them and the flood waters were lapping at the base of the hill not more than a block away.

Hunter moaned in his sleep, sat up suddenly and opened his eyes. A soft voice had awakened him, a voice that said a solitary word. *"Where?"*

He screamed, for there, standing in the middle of the darkened room was the woman he had murdered, Frieda James! Her face was luminous, even the clinging robe she wore cast off a ghastly light. He could see the blotches on her throat, could see the trickle

He looked up from where they had him bound. A woman was tossed in.

of blood flowing from her mouth. A finger pointed straight at him, a purple mouth said again, "Where?"

Lita Strawn encircled him with her arms, said, "What is it, dear? There's nothing here, no one here but me. You've been having a nightmare!"

FOR the rest of the night he cowered shivering and trembling while she did her best to comfort him. Once she turned on the lights and poured him a drink. He forced himself to peer fearfully over his shoulder. There was no one in the room but Lita. *But the next day, shaken and terrified, when he reached beneath his pillow for a handkerchief, a folded bit of paper fell from it. Lita opened it. There were three auburn hairs in the folded paper.* Even her eyes grew bleak and wide at the incoherent ravings that followed.

"We've got to get away, we've got to get away," were his final words, and she agreed that if he wanted to keep sanity, they must get away. But where?

It was Lita Strawn who managed someway to buy a boat with an outboard motor. And it was Lita who managed to get Hunter dressed and out of the hotel. Before leaving, she thrust a loaded revolver into his pocket. "Keep it," she murmured. "I don't know who or what is after you, but you may need it. I'm taking you to a place I know where they'll never find us, where we'll be safe."

They made their way through the crowded lobby of the hotel, stepped out into the mud and rain. From the height of the bluff, desolation was spread about them. For mile after mile the muddy yellow water stretched on every side. A block below, the business section of the town was completely inundated. In the grey of the driving rain he could not see far, but followed her blindly into the boat concealed at the bluff's edge. His fingers were gripping the butt of the gun so tightly they ached as the little motor roared into life and the boat bounded away into the yellow flood. Rain beat about them. She handled the boat like an expert, dodging floating logs, floating debris, and heading on into the dusk.

He never knew how long the ghastly journey continued. Presently the boat came to rest, and, peering ahead through the gloom and rain, he made out a knoll, raised slightly above the level of the flood. A few stunted trees loomed against the grey sky and behind them, a small house.

She grasped him by the arm. They sloshed through the wreckage and mud toward the dim house. "It's all right," she called above the roar of the water. "It's a caretaker's cottage that belongs to my husband. We'll be safe there and the flood will never reach us." His breath came in gasps as he climbed the slope. Mud sucked at his feet, gave with a gruesome sound as he tore them loose. Up across the stoop, the board porch. She left him at the door. "Go on in and light the lamp. I'll bring the stuff from the boat."

Inside he paused, lit a match. The roar of the turbulent waters was still in his ears. His nerves were jumpy as he fumbled for a match. Its flickering glare showed a lamp on a table in the middle of the room. He lit three matches before he succeeded in firing the smudged wick.

IN the very center of the table lay a white sheet of paper! And across the white sheet of paper were three hairs, hairs that gleamed like red gold in the pale light. Fascinated he stared at them, the old ache coming into his curved hands. A soft voice said, "Where?" *She* stood in the doorway, the same ghastly light playing over her mobile features. Her eyes seemed glazed, her mouth purple.

Slowly, slowly the gun came out of his pocket. "No, no," he gasped, "you're dead, dead!" The gun blazed, the rattle of the report filled the room. Presently he peered at her above the smoke of the empty gun. Her eyes continued to gleam, her body to cast off that eerie light.

She said, "Where?"

He screamed, threw the gun at her. It rebounded from the wall and she did not move. His sudden turn upset the table and the lamp crashed to the floor. Somehow he dove for her, felt his fingers sinking into the clammy flesh of her throat, felt the chill, deathlike moistness of her body. Then something descended on his head with sickening force, lights danced before his eyes, only to explode with a vivid flash and dissolve to nothingness as consciousness left him.

A HAND was slapping his cheeks, monotonously, stingingly. A voice was droning. "Come on, guy, wake up, wake up! There's things to do." He opened his eyes, stared at his tormentor.

He was a burly man with a flattened nose and a pugnacious jaw covered with heavy beard. His eyes were little, set far apart, bleak and hard.

"Who are you?" faltered Hunter. "What do you want? Where's Lita?"

The man laughed. "The dame? You want to see the dame? Okay, I'll bring her." He disappeared for a moment. Hunter tugged at his feet, tugged at his wrists, found he was bound upright in a

Suddenly he went berserk, knocking the girl down.

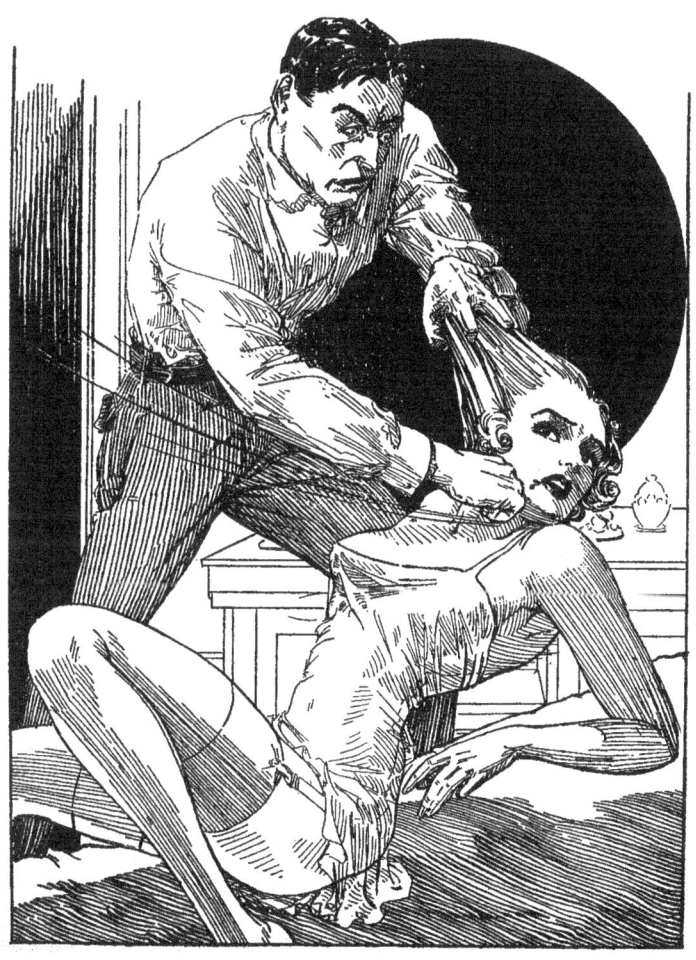

chair. The door flew open, Lita Strawn hurtled into the room, pushed by the newcomer.

Her dress was torn from her white shoulder, disclosing a long scratch above the quivering breasts. Her face was strained and white as she made for Hunter, moaning. The man at the door said. "I'll leave you love birds alone for a while. She'll explain, lug. Me and the boss will see you before you know it."

"Untie me," said Hunter shakily. "What's going on? I need a drink. I—"

"I'm afraid to untie you," she whimpered. "Listen, that's Bull Moroni and his boss is in the other room, Killer Dalls. They're the last of the Dalls kidnaping gang. I didn't know they were here. For the love of God, do whatever they ask! They'll torture us, kill us!"

Ten minutes later a sleek, well dressed man took her from the room. He returned followed by the flat faced one, Moroni. Killer Dalls, kidnaper, smiled at Hunter and there was no mirth in his smile. Moroni walked across the room, jerked Hunter's tie so tight that he strangled. As he loosened it and stepped back, Killer Dalls began to talk.

"That's what they do to murderers, Hunter. Listen, remember Belle Wharton? And Frieda James? Remember when you took Belle to Carsonville, Hunter? You got drunk and shot off your mouth. You told her about killing the James woman. You told her about stealing the money and the bonds. Now you've got one chance to save your life. Tell me where the bonds are."

A LITTLE at a time Hunter's addled mind began to clear. He was among his element now, he was with other criminals. This was Killer Dalls, another man. Just another shakedown. With something of his old spirit he said, "There were no bonds, Dalls. I took only the money."

Moroni said, "Should I clip him, boss?"

Dalls shook his head, smiled faintly. Without another word, the two men left the room, closing the door. Darkness was thick and heavy about Hunter. Outside the rain beat on the roof, pounded on the windows. Perspiration broke out on his brow.

Fear crept with hot feet through his veins. Something within him told what was about to happen and he died a thousand deaths.

SUDDENLY she was there. First blackness, impenetrable blackness. Then a nebulous lustre, a dead woman whose flesh and garments cast blue light, whose voice intoned one word over and over, "Where? Where? Where?"

He tried to fight down the fear, tried to tell himself these things couldn't be. But it was too much for him. His screams filled the room, the shrieks of a demented man, a man agonized by terror. The ghost of Frieda James disappeared. The door flung open.

"I'll tell, I'll tell!" shrieked Hunter. "I mailed it to myself at the Tremont in Kansas City! The package of bonds—I mailed it, I tell you. The insurance receipt is in my wallet, you'll find it there!"

DAWN came up over flooded wastes. A man cowered in a chair near the window of the deserted cottage. His eyes were alight with madness, his cheeks shrunken and covered with heavy beard. In his hand was clutched a sheet of paper. With unseeing eyes he tried to puzzle out the message it bore. The words danced and leaped on the page. He mumbled aloud:

"—so it may help your craven soul to know you didn't kill Frieda. You dropped your ring in the elevator and the janitor found it, recognized it. He took it to your apartment, heard Frieda threshing about inside. So her life was saved. I am Frieda's sister, the man you knew as Dalls is her brother. We knew we must get you some way without scandal, so when Belle Wharton came to Frieda, we bought information from her. She crossed you, Hunter. She was afraid of you. The rest you know.

"I don't think you'll try to make any trouble. Frieda is alive; she helped in the plan to frighten you, but you can still be held for attempted murder. You are a brave man with women, aren't you? But never forget that a woman broke you with a few strands of red hair, and a gun loaded with blanks. Anna Morgan. (Lita Strawn to you.)"

Somehow the script would not stand still for his feverish eyes to read. He gazed dully out the window at the raging water. The rain had ceased for the first time in weeks, but the waters were still rising. A sickly sun peered through the clouds, cast a feeble gleam through the splashed window. The letter fluttered to his feet. Dully he looked down, saw that muddy yellow water had crept up over the level of the door, had seeped into the house. Already it was about his ankles.

That intolerable ache was again in his hands, cramping them, hooking them like claws, talons. As if he had never seen them before, he peered down at them. And a strange laugh issued from his dry lips. *He had never noticed before that the hairs on his wrists and fingerbacks were tinged with red!*

Soon the sun disappeared again and the deluge resumed. Slowly, slowly the level of the water arose in the house. But John Hunter stared through the splashed window with unseeing eyes, eyes that were blank and vacant.

CLARK NELSON

FLESh OF ThE LIUING

*The job was a welcome one, both to the girl and the
man. She had been a model before; he was willing
to learn. But neither of them dreamed what would
be expected by the mad genius who specialized
in painting human emotions at their rawest.*

I'D *never been* drunk before in my life but that must
be what was the matter with me now. I wondered if there had
been some ingredient of unusual potency in the curious drinks
the woman, Marcia, had been ordering for me. I'd never tasted
anything just like them, and yet I hadn't thought it good policy
to ask. The woman, Marcia, with her curiously slanted eyes, had
just hired me for a job. And I couldn't chance displeasing her so
soon.

The ceiling of the cocktail bar at the hotel where I had met
her seemed to have taken on a motion of its own and, with an
effort, I brought my gaze down to eye level. I peered through the
blur that had come over my eyes at the other woman—the younger
one—Mildred I thought her name was—whom Marcia had
brought down to the bar with me. She seemed just as giddy as I
was. The smile on her face had become vague and meaningless,
and she appeared to be having trouble in keeping her head up.

I turned to my new employer, Marcia, and attempted by my
concentrated study of her to clear some of the cobwebs from my
brain. She was an exotic-looking, almost Oriental type. In her
uncanny eyes and in the whole manner of her bearing she seemed
unnaturally sure of herself. There was wisdom in her eyes that
might have required centuries in the planting; there was patience
reflected in the way she sat, as if she had endless time to watch
and wait for what was to come. But there was no hint that the
drinks had affected her.

Vainly I tried to bring sense into my befuddled mind. God

knows, I needed the job. It had been months since I had worked and I needed money badly. I tried to review the events of the day as an aid to clear thinking.

There had been the advertisement in the papers, specifying little about the type of work offered, but going into details about the physical requirements of the man wanted. And they had fitted me to a T.

Then there had been my trip to the hotel where I had met the woman, Marcia. She had hired me within five minutes. At the cocktail bar I had been introduced to the lovely younger woman, Mildred. And then there had begun this astounding series of rounds of fantastic drinks.

Into my thoughts there kept coming the premonition that there was something gruesome, something mysterious about to happen, but I tried not to think of it.

IT was becoming increasingly difficult for me to concentrate. Mildred, I saw, was frankly sleeping now. I turned back to Marcia with her peculiar eyes. There was no conversation. She just sat there, sipping her drink and eyeing me with the fixity with which a cat will watch a mouse-hole.

It was just about at that moment that nature intervened and managed a black-out for me. I tried to ward it off by standing for a moment but I was aware that what I was saying was stupid, and I sat down and put my elbow on the table and rested my chin in my palm.

Through a rift in the fog I saw the dark man who appeared from nowhere in chauffeur's uniform and took my arm. Marcia had Mildred's arm. The four of us made our way to the street exit through aisles of amused drinkers. I tried to show my indignation but knew I was not being successful.

I transferred my attention to the undulating hips of Marcia ahead of me. That woman was built with all the rippling muscularity of a cat. Stepping carefully, I tried to match my stride to hers. Already I had begun to fear that my weakness under the influence of the liquor might react unfavorably on the job on which so much depended. The thin dress that Marcia wore ac-

centuated every pro-
vocative contour of
her sleek body as she
half-supported
Mildred, and should
have been enough to
sober the world's
worst drunkard, but it
did little to help me.

At last we were on
the street. A huge
limousine waited and
my guide steered me
into the back seat
between the two
women. I was aware
of the pressure of a
firm thigh on my
right where Marcia
sat. On my left, where
Mildred sat, soft
curves flattened
against my side and
her head dropped on
my shoulder. Even
that wouldn't awaken
me. And then the
curtain came down in
earnest.

I AWAKENED
slowly, my head
feeling as if a crew of
boiler-makers were
working inside it. Al-
though it had been
early evening when
we left the hotel, we

*Horror lit in her eyes and a tremor
ran the length of her body when she
saw what was expected of her.*

were now speeding through dark night.

Only Mildred was in the back seat with me, and she was slumped in the far corner with her dress worked half off one shoulder, and ridden high above her knees. Gleaming white skin showed above the hem of her skirt and beneath the normal neckline of her bodice. Another time I might have been intrigued but now I felt nothing but vague pity. I leaned over and pulled down her skirt and drew the sliding sleeve back into place.

My glance went to the front seat where Marcia now sat beside the uniformed driver. He was handling the steering wheel with only one hand and the other arm around his exotic companion's shoulders. Gradually he slowed the car beside the road and pulled up. Then the two figures drew closer and I could see that Marcia was pulling the chauffeur's face down to her mouth.

There was still a haze obscuring my vision which probably accounts for my slow reflexes and complete inaction during what followed.

I thought I caught the gleam of metal but wasn't sure. Then I saw the woman's hand reach high above the chauffeur's back and shoulders and I saw it plunge down three times. For an instant his hands groped futilely for her face, but the third time his body slumped out of sight below the back of the seat. He moaned weakly; there was a gurgling sound; then quiet.

Like a flash, Marcia was out the door on her side. Another second and she was jerking the door open on the other side. I was aware of her dragging the slain man out into the night but still I was powerless to move. For the first time I realized that I wasn't drunk. I had been doped! Then I lurched over, my head on Mildred's lap, and I slept again.

THE next time I awoke, I knew I was on a bed, and I was in somebody's house. I heard the buzz of voices around me, but I was careful not to open my eyes. I lay there, faking sleep, but listening.

"Where'd you get him?" a man's voice asked.

"He was the pick of those who answered the ad," Marcia's voice replied. "He'd almost do as a double, except for his face, but that doesn't matter."

The man laughed and threw a bright flashlight's rays into my face. "No, the face won't matter," he said. Cold hands worked on me, feeling my muscles, testing my joints as if I were a captive in an old-time slave market. I realized then that I was practically naked.

The man continued: "Has he no people, nobody who'll miss him?"

"The girl and he are both strangers in the east. We're safe on that score."

Again the fingers began probing my muscles. I rolled suddenly aside, opening my eyes, but at that moment the light went out. I heard feet retreating hurriedly. I heard a door slam and a key turn in a lock, and I knew I was alone.

I fought my way to my feet, found the light switch. The door wouldn't budge. Then, for the first time, I had a chance to look around. The bedroom I was in was magnificently furnished. I caught a glimpse of myself in a full length mirror, only to discover that my sole attire was a brilliant purple loin-cloth.

For some reason, that fact made me more angry than all that had gone before. Where were my clothes? I rummaged around fruitlessly. In the room's closet I found a man's dressing robe, a bright yellow, quilted and obviously expensive. It was better than nothing. I put it on just as I heard the knock on the door.

Before I answered, a lock turned. A turbaned Indian entered drawing a serving table, laden with dishes.

I intercepted him as he bowed and started to move out. "Where are my clothes?" I demanded.

He was very suave. "They are being cleaned and attended to. Meanwhile you will want something to eat before the master, Astoll, sees you." He started once more to leave.

But my mind was a muddle and I had to know more. "Where am I? I guess I was drunk, because I don't know."

He was very patient with me. "You are at the home of Bernard Astoll, the painter. When he is ready to see you, he will explain everything." He paused as if choosing his words. "While you slept on the way out, perhaps you dreamed that Marcia and your driver had a disagreement?"

I WAS wondering what to answer when Marcia's voice spoke from the doorway.

"I think, Ali, that you needn't ask that. I'm sure our guest knows that I drove the car out, that the driver remained in town on an errand for Astoll."

Ali bowed and walked out, making no more noise than a cat. I pulled the robe together and eyed the slant-eyed woman. She returned my stare calmly.

I said: "Why bother to lie? I saw you kill our chauffeur." I jumped up from the table. "Whatever sort of mess this is, I don't like it. Send for my clothes. To hell with your job! I want to get back to town. And the girl that you introduced as Mildred some-thing-or-other—I think I'd better take her back with me."

"Eat and drink your wine!" Her voice carried all the insistence of the crack of a whip. Her eyes blazed fire and they had an in-tensity that seemed to stab with hypnotic fury. I was sure then that Marcia was mad. There seemed to be nothing that I in my still bewildered state could do just then.

I sat back at the table and ate and drank the heady wine in great gulps. My brain was in a whirl.

Her words, surcharged with venom, went on remorselessly. "You know you were drunk when you came out here. No one is responsible for any hallucinations you may have had. Actually, you saw nothing out of the ordinary, and you heard nothing!"

I raised my eyes from the table and looked at her. Again I cringed under her terrible gaze. I could scarcely tear my glance away from those slotted pits of evil. Her pupils were distended until they seemed to cover the whole eyeball.

Watching them, I hardly noticed the rest of her pantherish figure; her slender feminine waist arising above matured hips to the tempting swells of her breasts, to that white throat, so fragile looking but so firm and perfectly shaped.

Almost against my will, I found myself repeating, "I was drunk and I saw nothing and I heard nothing."

She gave a little laugh then and took the chair opposite me. She was like a different person.

"Eat all you want," she said. "Bernard Astoll, the artist, will interview you very soon. Do what he says and you'll have no trouble. I meant to tell you in the city, but may have neglected it that your job is that of model. Astoll is painting some murals and he commissioned me to find him the models he needed—you and the girl who came out here with you. Later this evening he is having guests. You two will join the rest as equals in every way. Mingle with them freely. It will give him a chance to study you in positions of relaxation. But eat and drink now. The night ahead is likely to be pretty busy."

THEN she was gone. And I, God help me! turned to the refreshments that had been served me. The food was too rich for more than a few mouthfuls but the wine was pleasant and invigorating.

Once more there was a knock at the door. This time slant-eyed Marcia brought Mildred, my companion on the back seat of the limousine.

She looked different to me this time. Whether it was the Chinese kimono that she held around her or not I don't know. The garment might have been made to order for her, so deftly did it enhance every line of her exquisite body. Her eyes seemed somewhat blood-shot but she contrived a wan smile.

There was another knock at the door barely after the two women had become seated. Marcia called and Ali, the turbaned, dark-skinned servant entered, bearing something—whether man or boy, I couldn't be certain at once—in his arms. He deposited his burden carefully in a big, comfortable chair, and I saw then that it was a deformed man, a hunchback who was almost a monstrosity, that he had brought in.

From his attitude and that of Marcia I knew at once that this was Bernard Astoll, the artist whom they had called the master. His head was enormous and completely hairless; his tremendous bowed shoulders were padded with bulging muscle; his nose was a huge amorphous bulb; his eyes tiny and penetrating. But when he moved his superbly beautiful hands, you forgot all the rest of his incredible ugliness.

They were long fingered and beautifully shaped, a little feminine perhaps, but unquestionably the hands of an artist.

He gestured with them now as he addressed Mildred and me. "Don't let my uncouth appearance alarm you, my friends," he said softly, and with a gentle chuckle. "God enclosed me in an unattractive earthly envelope, but, I assure you, he endowed me with a soul that is just as beautiful and as precious as your own."

I glanced at Mildred and saw the horror in her face, but my attention was at once drawn back to Astoll, who continued talking.

"I have been ill and am not yet strong enough to paint, so for a time your duties will be easy. You will live here at my house, and I shall try to make you comfortable until such time as I am able to go on with my murals. Once they are finished, you will be well paid and may go. At present I must keep you at my beck and call. But, first of all, I must know what sort of models Marcia found for me."

Now he addressed Mildred alone. "Take the dais, please."

I hadn't noticed before the model's stand in one corner of the room. It stood about three feet high, was draped with a rug, and the wall behind it was covered with black velvet. Astoll signaled and Ali dimmed the room's lights. A moment later he pressed another button that shot a spot light of dazzling intensity across the stand.

The hunchback addressed Mildred again. "I understand you have been a professional model. Our other young friend can watch you and learn what he must do next."

Wordlessly, but I could sense that she was shaking with fear, Mildred got up and stepped into the glare of the spotlight. Her back to us, she shrugged the kimono off so that it dropped in loose folds at her feet.

Under the golden gleam of her hair her skin was miraculously white. Her figure was like that of which men have always dreamed, straight and slim and magnificently feminine.

I caught my breath; Ali exhaled sharply; Astoll seemed to be purring. Slowly the girl turned, a living picture of grace and beauty.

Under the sculptured column of her throat, the lines of her breasts were proud poems of loveliness against the black back-drop. Her flat waist broadened into splendid hips, then tapered into firmly rounded thighs, exquisite calves, dainty ankles. That she was proud of her beauty she manifested in the perfection of her carriage as she pivoted slowly.

"That will be all," Astoll said after a moment. He turned to me. "Now it's your turn, please."

I hesitated only a second. After all, the man was a world-renowned artist. The woman Marcia was his confidential secretary. And I needed the money more than I liked to think.

I stepped up on the dais and dropped my robe. Clad only in loin-cloth, I stood, flexed my muscles, turned in various poses. In the brightness of the light I could not see the others and the job was less embarrassing than I had expected.

The lights came back on and Astoll indicated that he was tired but satisfied. Again wearing the robe, I stepped down and was immediately disquieted by the intent, calculating look on Marcia's face. She stepped near me, put a hand on my right arm, and squeezed my biceps. All the time those strange eyes of hers searched my face. The point of her red tongue moistened her lips, but she said nothing.

"I expect everyone downstairs within half an hour," said Astoll. "My guests have already begun to arrive." Ali carried him away.

Marcia took Mildred's hand. "We'll meet you at the foot of the stairs," she said to me.

"But I need my clothes."

"It's a costume party and you are dressed the way Astoll wants. You won't have to stay long. You'll find the rest of the party in costume, too." The two women left.

THERE seemed to be nothing I could do about it but this insane place was getting on my nerves. If I hadn't needed the money so badly, I would have put up more of an argument. As it was, I poured myself another drink of wine, and followed the others.

As I came to the head of the stairs, I was conscious of the music coming up from below, soft and sensuous, exciting and provocative. I started to go down and almost fell over the huddled white figure that crouched at the landing. I bent over her.

"Is something wrong, Mildred?" I was genuinely concerned.

She had been crying and now she moaned pathetically: "I'm scared. What's it all about? Why did I ever get into this?"

I patted her bare shoulder reassuringly. "That's silly. You've posed for artists before. There's nothing to be afraid of."

"But I *am!*" she persisted. "Have you seen this?"

There was a black velvet drape against the wall which I hadn't noticed before. Now she pulled the yellow cord that hung before it and it parted, uncovering an almost life-size painting.

At first glance, I recoiled in horror. The painting was undoubtedly the work of a great artist, but it was the most terrible thing I had ever seen.

I slid a comforting arm around Mildred's waist while I studied the picture. It seemed to have been conceived to portray symbolically the very epitome of physical pain.

In the background there stood a nude man lashed cruelly to a crude cross. From head to foot his body was a mass of unspeakable lacerations, as if a fiend had carved him slowly with a knife. His head was thrown back in an attitude of supreme agony; his eyeballs were rolled so high that only the whites of his eyes were visible; his mouth was tortured, flecked with foam. His right hand stretched out as if pointing, except that in place of fingers there were only five bloody stumps.

In the foreground of the painting, a woman, young, slender, extremely blonde was chained to a rock of some gleaming black metal. She was nude and so realistically painted that her flesh seemed to pulse with life. But, most important, she was actuated by a species of terror so profound that she seemed literally to be screaming. My very ear-drums vibrated to the intensity of that painted shriek!

Leaning over her was the figure of a torturer whose knife was sliding across her torso, creating streamers of blood that gathered in a pool at her feet. And the figure was of the painter himself—the terribly misshapen body of Bernard Astoll!

On a silver plate at the bottom of the frame was the picture's title, "Agony."

An involuntary shudder shook me. I reached for the yellow cord and the drape came together again, hiding the painting.

I HAD almost forgotten Mildred in the emotions that had taken hold of me while I had scrutinized the canvas. Now I turned to her and found her huddled at my feet, tossed by sobs. Fear grew in me—fear for myself as well as the girl. Was the picture of "Agony" some sort of portent of what awaited us?

I stooped and picked the girl up and cradled her against my breast and tried to stop her crying with my kisses. She trembled like a child in a nightmare and I could feel the ripples of her panic as they communicated themselves to me. I started back, looking for a side exit where we could go while we planned our next move, but Marcia turned up from nowhere, blocking our flight.

Her uncanny eyes were full of fire again but her smile was calm and assured. "Astoll has sent for you. His guests want to meet you."

I think my teeth were chattering as I stood Mildred on her feet. "But that picture…."

She laughed and put a hand on my shoulder. "That picture? The one in the hall? You *do* need a drink. That's nothing—just one of Astoll's imaginative nightmares."

She had me hypnotized again. Her fingers slid down my arm to my wrist and I was powerless to resist. We had just reached the staircase when I thought of Mildred and turned. She was following us but none of the horror had gone out of her eyes.

From below, clouds of incense and smoke arose to assail our nostrils. Soft music throbbed sensuously. For a moment I was conscious of nothing else except the dim figures of dancers. As my eyes accustomed themselves to the scene, I could see that these dancers were garbed like the dwellers in a monastery with cowled heads and long grey robes. Every face was masked but I could make out the gleam of eyes staring curiously our way.

I had been told that it was to be a costume party but somehow the fact that these people were all costumed alike and so completely that I could not tell the men from the women had a disquieting effect.

Then across the room I made out the deformed figure of Bertram Astoll. And at the same time some one snatched the yellow robe from about my shoulders. I turned and saw the curiously slanted eyes of Marcia. It was Ali, just behind her, who now held my robe.

Marcia shoved me gently and then I found Mildred by my side, timorously slipping her hand into mine. Together we approached the throne-like chair of our artist host and employer.

The music had changed in tempo now. As we walked forward the dancing people stopped dancing and made a path for us. Now and then a feminine hand would reach out to touch my arm or brush my thigh but, each time that I whirled, I would see only another pair of blazing eyes through the slits of a mask, and maybe the tip of a restless tongue licking at heavily made-up lips.

WE reached Astoll who sat deep in his chair, clad in a robe of imperial purple. He smiled a twisted smile that I think was meant to convey a welcome. Then the music sank until it was almost lost, and at that moment his voice came, high and shrill:

"My friends, I give you Beauty!"

Simultaneously a bright spotlight flashed out from high above us and bathed Mildred and me in its warm glow. I know that I turned red and I could feel the tremor that ran through Mildred's length as she pressed closer to me. The light changed in color, then changed again: blue, silver, salmon—color after color until it had run through the whole spectrum. And always I could feel the feral eyes of the robed figures as they slowly tightened the ring that surrounded us.

Suddenly the spotlight went out and hands fell on my wrist and shoulder pulling me backward. I whirled and saw the dark face of Ali. At the same time I caught Marcia's whisper. "Don't be frightened. It's a game. Just stand against the wall and be quiet."

I stood there tensely, back to the wall, but I noticed that Ali never left my side.

Now Mildred was all alone before Astoll's throne. He was

whispering to her, but I could not make out what he said. A curtain drew back behind him and a gigantic negro, clad only in loin cloth stepped out. In his hands he held a tray, covered with a golden cloth, which he put down at the artist's feet. Bowing, he backed away until he stood, arms folded, behind Astoll's chair, looking like a figure from the Arabian nights.

Astoll spoke softly to Mildred again. The robed figures closed in more and more.

Bewilderment manifested in her whole being, the semi-nude figure of Mildred dropped to its knees before the tray. She touched the cloth of gold, then abruptly lifted it from the tray.

For a moment the silence was absolute. Then Mildred's scream of horror filled the room, echoing and reechoing from every corner. I tried to move forward, but Ali's hands were on my wrists again like bands of steel.

By straining I could peer over the wall of monk-like figures. Mildred crouched in livid terror, one hand over her mouth, her eyes like those of one gone mad. And on the tray lay the head of one who must have died in excruciating agony, a head that reposed in half an inch of rich, red blood.

Once more Astoll's voice cut into the silence. "You have now seen my masterpiece, 'Horror'!" he exclaimed. "An unforgettable picture that no one but I could paint."

The giant black man came gravely forward and carried away the tray with its unspeakable burden. Marcia, too, stepped into the light and led Mildred, whimpering from the room. And still I found myself unable to shake off the grip of Ali's hands.

ONLY when Marcia reappeared, did he relax. Then not knowing what to do or which way to turn, I let her draw me after her from the room. We stopped in an alcove, steeped in a heady incense, where she drew me down beside her on a softly cushioned couch. She put a drink into my hand which I gulped automatically. It burned through me with a rich, invigorating glow, but still I couldn't put from my mind what I had just witnessed.

"Why does he do it? It's bestial!" I demanded.

"He hurts nobody," she replied. "It's mostly an illusion. But, you see, his guests tonight are wealthy patrons. He shows them the painting that he means to do. If any of them likes the scene, he bids for the finished work. Astoll's photographic memory permits him then to create it with no further posing."

The influence of the drink was rising in my veins. Already I knew it was lulling my more honorable senses. "What about Mildred? Where did you take her?" I asked.

"Don't worry. She's asleep in her room. Tomorrow she'll think no more about her experience tonight than she would of any passing nightmare."

I looked at her, trying to guess if she were telling the whole truth. Her long grey robe was gaping at the throat line. One long, slender, gleaming white leg had emerged from its folds and was lightly pressing my own knee. I could glimpse the rise and fall of her breasts with her breathing. Her warmth and her perfume were working spells on me.

I drew farther away.

"Afraid?" There was a taunt and a challenge in her voice, but more than that, the magic of those steady, exotic eyes had me half bewitched.

Still I tried to keep my senses. "Who wouldn't be afraid after what I saw in the car on the way up here!"

She laughed as if I had told a joke. "You know you were drunk," she said.

Even then I had a shred of caution, but like a fool I poured myself another drink. Then I was aware of her hand on my knee and her breath on my cheek. I could see the luminosity of her velvety smooth skin. Her arms lifted and slid their sinuous way around my neck. I glimpsed the flecks of fire in her eyes as her mouth came down on mine.

The soft music from the main ball-room was doing its part. The wine dulled my vision and my hearing, it seemed, but did not completely deaden my senses....

I WAS hardly conscious that the lights were getting brighter. And certainly did not see that a ring of peering eyes behind masks was closing in. I responded to nothing beyond something primitive deep within me.

I came back to the world at the sound of Astoll's voice.

"The most fundamental and universal of all the stirrings of mankind," he said. "I shall paint it in all its pagan simplicity."

I staggered to my feet trembling, aware of the gleams from the eyes around me. I looked down at Marcia whose mouth was contemptuous, whose eyes held a sort of unholy derision. Against the black velvet cushions she looked white and fragile but infinitely evil.

I know I swore at her then, and my hands darted for her throat. They sank into soft flesh and squeezed. The lights in her eyes changed and her own hands were on my wrists, but it was as if they were caressing me and not trying to break my hold. I think I went momentarily mad then. My fingers tightened even more. Her lips still smiled up at me when something came down on the back of my head with such force that I saw a flash of blinding light, then nothing.... I came to with a pounding inside my head, with the acrid odor of smoke in my nostrils. I tried to move to ease the pain that wracked my body and discovered that both my wrists and ankles were bound. I opened my eyes while my brain slowly cleared. Only then did I realize that I hung suspended from a crude cross.

My eyes began to focus about the room. Directly before me I saw a rock of some gleaming black metal, and lashed to it, the agonized figure of poor Mildred. I know I screamed a demented scream, and the sound of Mildred's shriek mingled with my own. The two of us were reenacting the horrible painting we had seen only a few hours ago.

Through a door came the turbaned Indian, Ali. I renewed my screaming and straining against my bonds. Ali didn't even glance up. On a table he laid a curved knife and a pointed iron. He blew with a bellows on a charcoal brazier, and thrust the iron into the red-hot coals. He went out, as business-like as he had come in.

THEN I saw Marcia. She flowed in now, clad in a filmy robe that accentuated every feminine curve. Her eyes were fixed, her mouth half-smiling. And, looking at her, despite the pain I was in, I realized suddenly that she must be a drug addict. She came up to within inches of me and bent and put her moist, warm mouth on mine.

"The others will be here soon," she purred. "And one of them will buy the picture. But I shall have the living tableau!"

She thrust out a hand, talon-like, and I could feel it tear the skin of my chest, could feel the blood follow in the wake of her nails. She laughed and leaned and kissed me again and again.

Then suddenly she whirled and snatched up the knife from the table. I know that I screamed again and heard Mildred's scream even above my own. Marcia whirled toward me, and, as she did so, there came a beating and a hammering and a shouting at the door.

Marcia stopped short and then leaped for the door. She jerked it open with knife upraised. It was the giant negro who tottered in, clutching at his breast. "The police! It's the police!" he gasped and collapsed in a heap.

Quickly Marcia barred the door and bent over him as his life-blood gushed out through the bullet-wound in his chest. "It's that damned chauffeur," he managed. "You never killed him!"

"I did!" she contradicted him. "I put a knife in him and left him in the swamp." But he didn't hear her. He was dead.

She leaped back to my side. "I can still have my living picture," she muttered. The knife flashed and I felt it rake my ribs. Once more there was a pounding on the door. "It'll hold until I finish," she gloated. "Then the three of us will go to hell together."

Her knife pointed toward my hand that was tied to the cross—and I thought with a shudder of the five bloody stumps in Astoll's painting.

The blade bit slowly into my fingers and as it bit I could feel her lips pressing just as fiercely on my mouth.

OVER her head I saw the spectre. Smoke still swirled from the brazier but I could see it. It was the chauffeur she had killed and he held an up-raised monkey-wrench.

Marcia's intuition then made her sense danger. She spun around and, as she did so, her razor-like knife slit through the ropes that held my right arm. But she was too late to save herself. There was a crunch as the wrench met her skull.

She stumbled and collapsed, but even as she fell she lashed out once with the knife and buried it in the chauffeur's throat.

With one arm free, I hastened to complete the job of freeing myself. And I was untying Mildred as the door crashed open. Half a dozen lovely blue-coated policemen thundered in. One of the last of them had Ali handcuffed to his wrist.

A detective looked down at the figures of the chauffeur and Marcia. "Boy, they sure hated each other!" he marveled.

"Hated, or loved?" asked Ali philosophically. "They were married; she tried to kill him; he brought the police. Hated or loved?" He shrugged.

I gathered Mildred into the circle of my arms. "There will be no question in our case, will there, honey?"

She didn't need to speak to answer.